'The story of a woman strong mind and make her own decisions when she knows they are the right ones. I loved this book, there are so many parts that will touch your heart and make you think about your own decisions. It takes you on a journey from sympathy to understanding, via laughter and tears, and ending with happy ever after, what more could you ask for?'

Katharine Gore

'This is a book that will make you laugh and cry along with Tabby. I thoroughly enjoyed every page and read it in one sitting. Something for everyone.'

K. Hensman

'A wonderful book that leaves you feeling warm and in tune with the world and its powerful force as well as relating well to the characters.'

Anzie

'My wife loved this book she read it really quickly and couldn't put it down. Giggles and happy tears what more can she say about it...decide for yourself and go buy it.'

Kiera

'Nicky has written a semi-autobiographical account of a young lady who is unhappy with her life. When her heroine discovers she has a psychic ability, everything changes. I loved the chapter about her discovering how to work with the Elements, that made me chuckle! It is an honest account of the trials and joys of modern life & motherhood.'

Mary English

# Tabby Turns The Tables

Nicky Marshall

Published in 2021 by Discover Your Bounce Publishing

www.discoveryourbouncepublishing.com

Copyright © Nicky Marshall

All rights reserved.
Printed in the United States of America & the UK. No part of this book may be used, replicated or reproduced, stored in a retrieval system, or transmitted in any form or by any means, electronic, mechanical, photocopying, recording, or otherwise, without the written permission of the author(s). Quotations of no more than 25 words are permitted, but only if used solely for the purposes of critical articles or reviews.

ISBN 978-1-914428-02-9

Although the author and publisher have made every effort to ensure that the information in this book is correct at the time of going to print, the author and publisher do not assume and therefore disclaim liability to any party. The author and the publisher will not be held responsible for any loss or damage save for that caused by their negligence.
Although the author and the publisher have made every reasonable attempt to achieve accuracy in the content of this book, they assume no responsibility for errors or omissions.
The content of this publication is purely fiction. Names, characters, places, and incidents either are products of the author's imagination or are used fictitiously. Any resemblance to actual events, or locales, or persons, living or dead, is entirely coincidental.

Page design and typesetting by Discover Your Bounce Publishing

# ACKNOWLEDGMENTS

I would like to thank my family and friends for the comments and support during the creation of this book and their love in real life. Also, a thank you to our amazing 'Team Bounce' at Discover Your Bounce Publishing.

# DEDICATION

To Ami and Kassi-Jayne, never doubt the existence of magic.

## DEAR READER,

This book is a fictional story of a character called Tabby. The book tracks her life, through its highs and lows as she learns about herself, her life and the Universe.

As with all stories, there must be influences taken from real life and this book is no different. It is up to you, dear reader, to decide to what extent this is true.

I hope you find this book an enjoyable read and that by sharing the life of Tabby you can see that with a little energy and the help of the Universe, anything is possible!

Nicky x

# INTRODUCTION

Tabby took one look at Casper's face and knew he'd done it again.

At any moment her friend would turn around to look for the socks belonging to her newborn and firstborn. Once again she would have to apologise and inwardly cringe at the obvious lack of discipline of the lovable, big-eyed Springer Spaniel, who was currently lying stage left with a bulging mouth.

There just seemed to be one embarrassment after another recently. If it wasn't one of the girls forgetting their permission slip for that all important school trip, it was sending in shop bought rather than homemade cookies for the cake sale.

Tabby had been blessed with a bright mind and a great sense of humour, but her ability to imitate Delia Smith was going to take some work. As for those forms, well the school secretary would just have to be patient!

It wasn't as if she had any grand ambitions for life. She always dreamed of bringing up a family and owning her own home. Her parents had done a great job giving her happy memories of family holidays and Sunday mornings dancing around to the radio.

She went straight from school into a banking job, safe with the knowledge that this would be a step towards achieving her dreams. It seemed quite uncanny that the first mortgage payment was exactly the amount of her salary and that continued to happen quite naturally every month, even when the girls arrived and the bank had to be part-time, a few promotions meant magically that hallowed mortgage that she had aspired to paying out of her own money still got paid.

Snapping back into reality she realised that not only did Casper have the socks, but he would never give them back even with the 'assertive' voice she had learned at dog training. Some things in life are so certain that she did what she did best: filled the kettle for tea and life carried on.

****

# CHAPTER 1

From her teenage years Tabby had always known she was different. This was usually put down to her Piscean nature and overactive imagination. People joined in willingly with her antics and ideas as she was easy going and laughed a lot.

Growing up, she loved to be the first one to find new things and the one you could always dare knowing it would be done. From immensely tight pin-striped jeans to flowing silk shirts that reached her knees, she always wanted to be the first one to step out.

Life in Tabby's world could be a little unpredictable – when something needed to happen it had to be now! Sometimes these happenings were fun and full of laughter and at other times the results were a little catastrophic. Like the time when she craved beautiful blonde highlights in her dark brown hair. Her mother had promised to make her an appointment with the hairdresser, but that seemed like ages away! So, on a Saturday when she knew her parents were going out, she hopped on the bus into town and bought a highlighting kit. As soon as the car left the drive she called for Kimmy, her partner in crime, and the two set to work with tinfoil and a mixture of slimy dye. It was only after it was all off and they were blow-drying that the realisation dawned…the sophisticated blonde look took a little more time to develop and Tabby was left with streaks of orange.

Another occasion of note was when she found a recipe for milk fudge. Again it was spur of the moment and again Kimmy was involved. The pair bought the ingredients and dashed home, immediately grabbing bowls, spoons and saucepans, giggling and adding bits rather than weighing everything perfectly. The resulting fudge was very tasty…however her ears took a battering after her patient and caring mum scrubbed the saucepan for hours before admitting defeat and throwing it away.

At school Tabby had a great group of friends and spent her youth being part of a crowd. They all lived nearby so there were plenty of days at each others' houses or walking to the park. As the friends grew up, their trips were further afield and were usually in the pursuit of boys!

One afternoon in particular was spent at the local pitch and putt, where their giggles could be heard from afar as their failed attempts at playing properly resulted in lying on the grass curled up laughing helplessly. The group were sure the subject of their affections never knew they were being followed, a sweet thought but very idealistic as they had caused quite a stir!

The village where Tabby lived was a close-knit community, where everyone mostly knew everyone else. You couldn't get into much trouble without your dad finding out, but there was always space for mischief and adventure. There was never a trip anywhere that hadn't been with company though and everything was always in safe limits. Thinking back, she couldn't remember doing anything on her own.

It was while still at school that she met her future husband. She was sixteen when they started to go out and she seamlessly went from the care of her loving parents to the care of a besotted boyfriend. The couple had fun going out together, getting to know each other's families and laughing together. It was strange but even from the outset Tabby's friends seemed to realise that this was more serious than her previous boyfriends. They spent every day seeing each other, despite the 'it's too soon' looks from her concerned parents.

After going out for a couple of years it seemed obvious to get engaged, then married and soon they set up a home. They bought a house just over the river from her parents and quickly filled it with handouts from their families. Gradually, over time, they decorated room by room and bought some of their own furniture.

Tabby worked in the local bank and enjoyed the social atmosphere and interaction with people. At times she wondered why she had always wanted to work in a bank; after all she had been pants at maths in school. Each lesson was spent trying to get Mr Grace, their teacher, off his chosen subject and she was well known as the one that could get a whole lesson covering the wonders of golf. It was only when her grades started to suffer that she realised this may not have been such a good plan after all.

She thought that the reason for her chosen profession was that her dad respected his bank manager, so working in the bank gave you respect and the label of being dependable. It also meant security; a steady wage so that she could afford a house with her husband.

The journey from teenage individual to respectable housewife happened without any conscious thought. At no point did she consider her future hopes and dreams. The idea of adventure and excitement and trying new vistas never even occurred to her. Now that didn't mean life wasn't fun; of course it was. Initially they spent hours working on building their home and there were giggles and parties as their friends and family helped with the DIY. They enjoyed holidays away, usually two weeks on a beach somewhere, as well as breaks with friends. Tabby loved her husband and remembered how initially she was excited and flattered as he fell head over heels in love with her and wanted to spend every waking hour in her company. He was unpredictable, headstrong and full of fun.

She settled into married life really well and loved playing house. It wasn't long before they decided to start a family and the couple were delighted to find out she was pregnant. When Liza came into the world Tabby was overjoyed. Adoringly she marvelled at those dark, intense eyes and Liza's perfect suntan. She felt a huge responsibility initially, worrying about whether she could support and look after this bright new soul. Her worries quickly ebbed away as she spent hours talking to her daughter, telling her about how life was going to be in the soothing voice reserved for babies.

Her husband had been overjoyed at Liza's arrival, dancing in the street at 2am on his way home from the hospital after the nurses finally persuaded him to get some sleep! He would change and feed her and walk around talking to his firstborn as she looked around her with interested eyes.

Tabby's world was one of domesticity, part-time working and coffee mornings. She loved being a mum and watching Liza learn and grow. She loved keeping her house nice and entertaining friends. Too soon it was time to go back to work at the bank and her mum delighted in looking after Liza. They would drop Tabby to work then drive to Tabby's grandparents' house. After work she would listen intently to any stories of the day and roll her eyes if Liza did anything new while she wasn't there to see.

Following in the loving footsteps of her mum, she went to great lengths to please others. She bought amazing gifts and arranged fantastic surprise parties for her family. She would get so excited preparing every detail of the surprises and would literally beam from ear to ear when the time came to reveal the secrets!

Often Tabby would stand back and marvel over how life had changed in a few short years. Leaving school at sixteen to becoming a mum a few days before her twenty-first birthday had been a huge transformation, but it felt so right. Sometimes there were worries of course, but generally the course of her life ran smoothly.

****

# CHAPTER 2

Tabby was dependable, likeable and fairly attractive in her eyes.

As with most women, there were always a few pounds to lose or a bit more effort to make, but no one really noticed if she made the effort. In fact, life was sometimes easier if she didn't make too much effort. With her husband being the jealous type, it was sometimes better to be invisible on a night out.

On the inside though, there had always been this space. This part of her that was quietly empty, almost sitting dormant. This silent, stagnant void that felt like it needed filling…but how? From time to time she wondered about it, but could never quite fathom what 'it' wanted.

Occasionally she allowed her imagination to wander off, usually while staring out of the window on a sunny day or watching the moon on a winter's evening. It was as if a part of her wanted open space, to walk barefoot, be free and do something different…but what? Was there this big secret in life that was somehow eluding her?

Tabby never spent any time on her own, had never even been out of her native city without company. Generally she was happy doing what she was doing, but if she did want to be alone, where would she go and what would she do?

When these thoughts got too confusing, which was often, she would snap back into reality. She would take a deep breath, count her blessings and remind herself of her beautiful life. She would say thank you for her lovely house and her fantastic family and go and find something constructive to do – usually the ironing!

This way of life had worked perfectly, to a point. But at the age of twenty-three it felt as if the Universe suddenly decided that was enough. Everything that had worked before suddenly ceased to. The results were so profound and ran so deeply that no one could have warned her of the turning tides around the corner. If they had, she simply would not have believed them.

When Tabby gave birth to her second child, a beautiful and healthy baby girl, she was overjoyed. In absolute awe she looked into the sparkly pools of blue that sat where Lauren's eyes should have been. This little miracle was all pink and wrinkly, and lovingly she marvelled at her…through a gas and air haze it was true!

It was only after a few hours of settling into the ward and getting comfortable that she realised they were alone. Gradually it dawned on her that her husband hadn't shared in her joy, preferring to grieve for the boy he didn't have.

The very idea that someone wouldn't want their child was inconceivable to her. She had spent the last ten, yes ten months talking to this baby, hoping that he or she would be healthy.

As her due date passed she had become more and more impatient, trying endless old wives' tales to hurry the birth along – to no avail! In fact it was a full five weeks after her due date that she had finally given birth. How could it be possible that at the moment your child arrives, after all that time, as a parent you could simply say, "No thanks."

So what are you supposed to do when the partner that shares your life opts out? Sharing the feeding and endless nappy changing was one thing, but what do you do when you suddenly realise you are in it alone?

Coping with the shock of this situation took some time. Tabby's gut told her to run, to take her children and not look back…but she had a newborn baby to care for. Her protective maternal streak was screaming in outrage, crying out for justice. Strangely though there was a quieter, calming voice that encouraged her to keep quiet. For some reason she listened to the quieter voice as it felt like this voice knew best and maybe had a bigger picture in mind.

Liza, now two, thought her younger sister was splendid and so mother and daughter set to work playing peek-a-boo and guessing what their new baby needed with each new cry. Generally, though the crying was infrequent and the young Lauren would look at both of them with her adoring eyes, even bluer now and complimented by a wisp of blonde hair.

After a few days her husband announced that he was 'ok about it' and ready to step into the role of dad. Outwardly Tabby smiled and accepted the statement, but she knew in her heart it was too late. The whole situation would have been enough to cope with had she had time to wonder what to do about it, but it seemed that life had other plans.

One day, when Lauren was just two weeks old, Tabby and her nan popped out to run a few errands while Liza was at nursery. She always appreciated her nan's support and was very grateful of someone to sit in the car while she popped to the bank.

They were out for less than an hour and had collected some chips once they picked Liza up. Getting Lauren from the car, her blood ran cold as Liza skipped back, still carrying the chips to declare, "Mummy, Grampy Jack's fallen over…"

Calmly she helped her nan to call an ambulance, rang all the relatives and stayed to lock up after the ambulance left. The news from the hospital wasn't too scary; her granddad had suffered a mild stroke and should be up and about relatively soon.

Over the next few days she made sure her nan had provisions for the hours she spent holding her beloved husband's hand. Running errands and organising came naturally to her. Her mum and nan spent their lives looking after other people, so Tabby thought of the things that others would forget. In between organising childcare, running to and from the hospital and looking after the girls, she would ensure that she was home in time to get the tea on the table and then deliberately switch her brain off and aimlessly spend the evening letting the TV distract her.

She did have one problem: trying to keep the news from her mum who was away in Lanzarote. Her nan had been very clear that her holiday was not to be interrupted as the stroke was mild. It was clear that Tabby had inherited her intuition from her mum who rang endlessly, knowing something was up. Everyone was thankful that this had been a mild stroke, and although her granddad could no longer speak they all hoped this would be temporary.

Tabby took Lauren into the hospital one afternoon and her granddad had held her. It was a magical and bittersweet moment as he wept silently, his eyes filled with joy at holding this beautiful soul in his arms. Although he couldn't speak, his eyes said everything. He had always been a man of few words, just happy and content to be with his family.

Her mum finally managed to get the details out of her after catching her in a weak and tearful moment and promptly made arrangements to fly home.

She arrived just after the second stroke, which had done much more damage. The waiting game began for the family; no one knowing how much longer her granddad would have in this world. Day by day his heart kept on beating, much to the surprise of the doctors.

Tabby hadn't felt able to visit after taking Lauren and decided this was for the best. In her head was the happy picture of her beloved granddad holding his great-granddaughter and that was the image that she wanted to keep.

All the rest of the family could do was hold his hand, stroke his cheek and say their goodbyes before the amazing man that they all loved so much quietly passed away.

Tabby's maternal family had always been extremely close, spending hours each week in each other's company drinking tea and giggling. While growing up she had always been at home in her grandparent's house; helping to make mountains of rock cakes while her patient nan smiled at the flour spilling everywhere and the spoon being licked. When her brother arrived she spent a blissful few days with her grandparents. Each morning there would be boiled eggs and soldiers on the sunny back doorstep, followed by TV watching and games and yet more rock cakes.

Throughout her teenage years Tabby always disappeared off to her nan's when her teenage rebellion had needed attention. The time when she 'left home' due to a (very minor) Sunday morning argument between her parents was a great example of this. After soothing words from nan, she would sit with her grampy who would give her a wink and tell her stories of his high jinks growing up in a small village. He always had hours to spare for his grandchildren, sitting in his chair watching as they played with Lego or stuck fuzzy felt. As they grew up their grandparent's house became the hub; the meeting place where they all caught up. There weren't massive displays of affection, but lots of dancing around the kitchen, shared parties and just a natural feeling of belonging that Tabby loved.

It was only natural that the whole family missed her beloved grampy and were all devastated. Her nan lost the man she had shared her whole life with, how do you get over that? She was a worker though, so daily the house still got tidied and the washing done.

She included her nan in looking after the children, pretending she needed the help. They both knew that she didn't, but that remained unspoken and along with her mum the two girls got cared for, kissed and hugged as they became the focus of the family.

The pain was visible on the face of Tabby's mum. Along with her dad, she kept an eye on her, allowing her quiet moments to walk out of the room when it all got too much and gently changing the subject when conversations got difficult. With her granddad no longer around, her mum assumed the role of organiser and became a tower of strength for her nan.

To grieve seemed impossible, Tabby had two small souls that relied upon her - how could she crumple up into a heap? So she hatched a great plan: she would carry on as if nothing had happened and life would go on. The waves of grief that threatened to engulf her were enormous and savage, there was no way she could give in to them and still remain in charge.

This plan seemed perfect and life carried on as normal. When people offered their condolences, she became artful at changing the subject. At the funeral she stared into space, refusing to acknowledge the coffin that held her granddad's earthly body.

Tabby collected her girls on the way to the wake, so she had no time for reminiscing or reminders of her grief. Day by day she threw herself into her children, her house and everyday life. Days turned into weeks as she doggedly got into a routine of normality that was a little too stringent but otherwise functional.

She was tight-lipped and held her grief bravely in check. Her rigid tidying up and slight agoraphobia were worrying to her closest friends, but she resolutely ignored the raised eyebrows and knowing looks as she plumped cushions and gave excuses. Her Health Visitor raised a few concerns, but Tabby's smiling eyes and distracting conversations were her saviour and her cut off, stony actions carried on undisturbed. This behaviour could have carried on forever.

Then the headache hit...

At first it was just a nagging daily headache that was a little distracting, but gradually the pain grew. When her headache reached its worst point there was nowhere to go to get distracted. Driving the car or working was impossible when your vision was disturbed and the pain intense. At first, she didn't think it was serious, but as time wore on her parents and the doctor became quite worried.

Tabby was positively furious with her body for being such an inconvenience. It seemed that the obvious solution was to reach for the painkillers and carry on as normal, however the pain never went and nothing worked. The ironing piled up and the dust settled and she continued to fret about the inconvenience.

On the inside there was a growing sense of panic that she couldn't fathom. She continued to demand different drugs and do her best to keep up with as much work as she could, while being confined to barracks.

Tabby sulked when the baffled doctor had suggested a

Cranial Osteopath as something to try. Holistic therapy wasn't something she was interested in, apart from a massage as a gift a few years ago which had been quite nice. What could a Cranial Osteopath offer that the drug conglomerates couldn't?

Grudgingly, after the headache got to its fourteenth debilitating week, she agreed. Although she had misgivings, she couldn't ignore her daily agony and anyway, her mum insisted. By now even looking after her children was sometimes impossible.

\*\*\*

It was in the first five minutes of her visit that Tabby realised she had made a mistake. This quiet, unassuming lady started off with some factual stuff and then ventured into forbidden territory: her emotions.

When her husband had rejected their beautiful second born, she had packed all the pain away into a box. When her beloved granddad had suffered his stroke two weeks later she had valiantly set about caring for her nan and swallowed yet more shock. With her parents away she had juggled breastfeeding every two hours with running to the hospital and ensuring her worry-stricken nan had provisions, putting her own feelings aside. When two weeks later her granddad had died there was yet more shock and grief to swallow.

It hadn't been a conscious decision to hide everything away; Tabby just decided that life had to carry on for the sake of her two daughters and became very busy. Once she had written herself a daily list, concerned herself with the tasks of the day and got into an exhausting routine it had been easy to dismiss any thought of emotion. As time had gone on she became an actress, effortlessly winning an Oscar or two every time anyone asked her how she was. The phrase, "I'm fine, how are you?" can be used as a brilliant deflection as long as the people around you expect you to be 'fine'.

It appeared that the lady sitting calmly in this peaceful space knew in an instant that she was far from 'fine'. After the first three questions, Tabby nearly bolted out of the door as her emotions bubbled up, desperate to be heard. With a deep breath, she took a timid step in the direction of healing and quietly lay on the couch.

The next few months were quite a rollercoaster. It seemed that emotions are great at getting to a safe middle ground when life gets too intense. A safe space where nothing is too painful, but the art of a good belly laugh becomes impossible too. Once Tabby's frazzled system had been reset by a few trips to this amazing lady, life became more and more interesting. One minute she would be ironing and the next tears would be silently falling down her weary face. Someone would tell her a joke that wasn't really funny and the next thing she would be laughing uncontrollably with even more tears. All she could really do was go with it – her head and logic had been in charge for far too long, and now her emotions had actioned a coup.

Days could be exhausting, but at least now the headache had departed and she just decided to give in, being too tired to fight any more. The sessions with the osteopath had been very enlightening; she learned a lot about how the body and emotions react. She'd been fascinated and a little scared at how someone as healthy and usually sorted as herself could get into such a state.

The holistic approach to life and wellness was an intriguing subject and Tabby wanted to know more…but for now recovery seemed to take up all her energy. A quick recovery was all that Tabby had planned, but it seemed her body had other ideas.

Once her headache went and her emotions started to settle a little, the next thing demanding attention was her tummy. The pain started as a rumbling once a month for a week or so, nothing major but a little more than her usual 'woman's problem.' This was a little frustrating, but she came from a long line of women with a high pain threshold and she got on with it. Soon though the pain became constant and the week long periods became three weeks long, something that Tabby knew wasn't normal. Eventually her mum convinced her to venture back to the doctors, where a few tests were carried out and exploratory surgery was advised. It appeared that the surgery would be straightforward and as she read the information she saw that some ladies elected to be sterilised at the same time…something she tentatively mentioned to her husband. He had been quite keen to try for another baby after Lauren arrived but while Tabby said nothing to the contrary, inwardly she knew there was no way she could have another child.

She had two daughters that continued to delight her every day, but what if a third child was also a girl? Could she really go through that anguish again? Could it be that her body was giving her a painful way out of saying anything? After months of painful periods and times when her husband had been called on to help with the ferrying of two busy children, it was agreed that a sterilisation would be the only option as more children would worsen her condition.

Her husband had been very reluctant, but Tabby's

insistence and determination must have shown as the doctors agreed it was possible, despite being twenty-seven and considered very young to be sterilised.

The surgery was very straightforward and only mildly uncomfortable. Her painful periods had obviously raised her pain thresholds. At the consultant visit she could only sit in shock as the ageing doctor said they couldn't find anything wrong. On a later visit to her GP her shock turned to outrage as she read the consultant's notes, stating that, "This stressed out housewife should learn to go home and calm down." The official test result: nothing wrong.

So, with no answers and no label for her condition, Tabby carried on with life. The children got to nursery even though the process of getting ready would happen while she crawled around on all fours. Standing up was too painful, especially early in the morning as her swollen belly continued to protest. The school run would be swiftly done and mostly she collected the girls – unless she found herself confined to the bath by the bleeding, at which point her mum would take over. It seemed her body quite liked being in charge and each day was a mystery; would there be hot flushes today – or as her mum called them 'personal summers' – or would the pain take over?

Her once colourful and fitting wardrobe became full of shapeless and elasticated garments as from morning to afternoon the bloating would take over. She practised smiling and being quite gracious in the playground as the mums asked when the next little one was due – after all who could blame them?

Her hems got longer and the jumpers more shapeless. Her fringe got lower and lower and her glasses got bigger as she continued trying to hide. It bothered her that she didn't have a reason for her pain or a diagnosis to cling to. She was sure there was something quite wrong going on inside of her, she felt so heavy and dragged down by it all…but the doctors had said it was nothing.

All the while though the house remained spotless, the tea got to the table and mostly life carried on. She watched her children grow and loved spending time chatting with them and watching their games.

Over the last few years her husband had become less and less attentive to the ups and downs in Tabby's life. Sometimes she would try to make an effort and arrange a night out. She would book her younger cousin to babysit with his girlfriend and do her best to look nice. Finding something to fit that looked feminine was tricky and heels inflamed the pain, but she was always up for a challenge!

## TABBY TURNS THE TABLES

When she was ready, she would make her entrance and ask, "How do I look?" Without actually looking up, her husband would reply, "Ok". The compliments usually came from their babysitters and in a bid to hide her disappointment, she would crack a joke and make light of her husband's blatant indifference.

\*\*\*

It was during these pain filled years that Tabby had discovered Casper, who quickly became the newest love in her life.

The girls loved having pets and they had always wanted a dog. Once they were in school and after weeks and weeks of nagging, pleading, big eyes and promises, she finally gave in and they paid a trip to a local breeder. Choosing which puppy was theirs was particularly tricky, but one tail wagging, bright-eyed and slightly shy bundle soon came home with the family.

Casper was supposed to be the family pet, but it soon became clear that he was here to give her the unconditional love and affection that she was missing. Those huge eyes watched her every move and he would happily follow her from room to room. When the girls were around, he delighted in playing with them with endless enthusiasm and suffered their cuddles and calling. When they were at school, Casper would quietly lie by her feet or try to sneak onto the sofa even though he knew he was banned. Casper had a penchant for eating socks and chewing the backs of shoes. The chewing he gradually grew out of after spectacularly eating the majority of the sofa, but the sock fetish was something he became famous for. He also loved to pull Tabby from the house, across the road and into the field in record time despite puppy training and one-to-one classes.

Another osteopath visit was in order to re-align her neck, but the pulling continued. With so many endearing qualities to his name, he was always forgiven for this shortcomings.

Although Casper's arrival was a group decision, it was clearly Tabby who had been assigned the walking duties, despite all of her husband's promises and intentions. Grey wet mornings and sunny afternoons saw her out and about and mostly she coped as she loved her new companion.

When the pain was particularly bad and her ashen face was filled with suffering, there was no reaction or sympathy to be had from her husband. As long as nothing interfered with life and routine and she was still able to make the Sunday 'in-laws' visit, plus the occasional trip out, all was well. But when this wasn't possible, on a day where the pain was too bad to hide and she asked for rest, there would either be sulking or she would be labelled as 'boring'.

A few years earlier she had been spirited, opinionated and fiery. She was passionate and would have been up for a fight and desperate to get her point across. It seemed this fighting spirit had now left, and unbeknown to Tabby, she was becoming numb and immune. Immune to the jibes and belittling comments, but also to any feelings of affection that were once held for the man she had vowed to love, honour and obey.

\*\*\*

At twenty-nine, after a chance meeting with someone sympathetic in the medical profession, she finally discovered an angel. After her mum had persuaded her to make one last trip to the doctors, it seemed a locum heard the desperation in her voice. Was it her imagination, or had this man been incensed about her treatment? Speedily she was referred on to another angel, who easily diagnosed the reason for her three years of constant pain and embarrassing misery.

Since her children were born, she had been suffering

from a severe prolapsed womb. She was shocked to finally have the answers. A hysterectomy was suggested, which seemed like a really big and final step. The surgeon very calmly asked her if she felt like a woman in her current condition, to which of course she said no. "So I suggest we change that," she said in a matter-of-fact way and wrote out the necessary paperwork.

The operation date quickly followed as she was considered an urgent case after years of suffering. The operation was scheduled just after Lauren's sixth birthday and her birthday trip to the zoo had been quite surreal for Tabby. As she looked in the mirror while getting ready, she really couldn't recognise this pain ridden, dragged down old woman in shapeless clothes with a tired expression.

The operation went smoothly and she woke up with a strange sensation: she felt no pain. Now it was time to start the lengthy recovery process, with weeks of no lifting while her tummy recovered.

The family adjusted to her being out of action, for a while. Initially the tea got cooked and the girls got fetched and looked after, but after a few weeks of her husband looking after her and getting lots of praise for it, the novelty wore off for him.

Mostly she found she could ignore the dust and the

washing piling up. On one occasion she gave in to her frustration and took a bin bag out after it had languished in the hallway for a week. As the colour drained from her face, she realised this had been a bad idea and after a weekend of agony she decided that she really needed to be good.

Looking in the mirror this time though, Tabby marvelled at how the body can cope with years of struggle. Overnight the pain that had etched into her face had fallen away.

Gradually and slowly, she recovered her ability to live a normal life and the calendar didn't have to be worked out with a plan A and a plan B. Once again she could take her children to the park, accompany them on a swim and walk them to school.

The simple things in life became a pleasure and she realised what a slog the last few years had been. It was strange coming to terms with years of struggle, she knew how hard it had all been and yet she couldn't quite accept that it had all happened to her.

It was at this point that she made another realisation, although quite what she would do about it she wasn't sure. Now that she had a body that worked and emotions that had found their equilibrium, she was able to look at her whole life.

Rather than purely surviving she now had other choices and could look into the future. Looking at the man who shared her life, she realised that there were no emotions for him.

No love, no hate, no passion, no excitement…just a sad realisation that life had changed to such an extent that she couldn't envisage growing old together like they had once talked about.

She had never considered herself to be a quitter though, so there were a few more years spent convincing herself that she could fix this.

There were holidays booked, babysitters arranged and hours of trying to make life different. The theme of being worlds apart continued throughout and the voice that spoke of there being more to life just got louder and louder.

****

# CHAPTER 3

Life was less than perfect in Tabby's world.

But now she had a space to fill that had previously been taken up by pain and illness. By this time the girls were both in school full time and continued to be the objects of her affection. After school times could now be occupied by activities as she had more energy, so the evenings were filled with ballet lessons, gymnastics and swimming…more things to be late for!

Her girls were very different and she marvelled at how two children born of the same parents could have such different looks, personalities that were poles apart and even eat completely different diets.

Liza had amazing chocolate brown eyes, beautiful dark hair and a European look. From birth she was on a mission to talk, walk and explore and she thrived in adult company. She was cute and giggled a lot and would always do as she was told providing you could explain why. When explanations weren't forthcoming Liza would show her dismay with a very dark and disapproving look!

When Lauren came along Liza beautifully adapted to being second mum to her sister and was protective and caring. Liza loved to chat to Lauren, who would just look up adoringly at her sister and hang on her every word.

When Lauren finally bounded into the world she also had amazing eyes, but huge and blue. She was a typical English Rose, with a pale complexion and a shock of blonde hair which grew into a spike that refused to be combed down. Whereas her sister was the explorer, Lauren was a laid back and chilled out baby, content to watch the world around her and smile at anyone who spoke to her. Lauren was in no hurry to crawl and spent her first few years at a sedentary pace.

Liza fussed over her food, Lauren ate everything. Liza loved chicken, Lauren loved tuna. Liza loved to read; Lauren would listen and then draw a picture. As each day passed more differences would become apparent, but they loved to play together and squabbles were infrequent.

Tabby had started accountancy studies when Lauren was a baby and continued her studies even while feeling poorly.

Once Lauren had started school she found a part-time job so her practical experience could grow too and gradually the job titles changed; Book Keeper grew to Accounts Assistant, which then became Assistant Accountant. Now she felt a bit better evenings were taken up with college and eventually home study.

Initially college was hard and something that took a while to get used to. She didn't view herself as academic by any means and had to drag her baby brain into numbers, essays and structure. She started to enjoy her studies though and one by one she passed exams and moved closer to her dream job.

This was a great distraction for Tabby, giving her a focus and a mission that she was determined to complete. There was still something missing though, an emptiness and a lack of...something. What would it take to fill the gaping hole where her emotions and marriage had once lived?

Once again though, the Universe had a plan.

She had always had a healthy fascination with the alternative world of tarot, the possibility of there being reincarnation and of the existence of ghosts and spirits. She'd been for tarot readings and a spookily accurate palm reading as a teenager had predicted her marriage to the month, even though at the time she had scoffed as it hadn't matched their original plan. She loved reading her stars in the papers and would trawl through spiritual magazines soaking up a bit of this and a snippet of that.

Anything esoteric would grab her attention and she was so curious about what else existed. As a teenager she loved to read Stephen King books and frighten herself silly at the storylines. She loved the thought that there was more to life and things that remained unexplained. Tabby never really thought that she would get the answers she was subconsciously seeking.

When Lauren started school her classmate had a familiar mum: Freda. Tabby went to school with Freda's brother who was a few years younger, so followed her on through secondary school. Freda had appeared quite scary then, with her wild hair and purposeful walk. She seemed to cut a swathe wherever she went and most of Tabby's friends stayed well clear of her too.

Later they both belonged to the same gym for a while and their daughters had shared the crèche, so she got to know Freda a little better. There was a surprisingly self-conscious, quieter side to her and a gentle nature that showed through once they got talking.

The gym didn't last very long in her chaotic life and so they had lost touch, but now here was Freda at the school gate every day, smiling and having a chat, and she inwardly marvelled again at the coincidental meeting. It wasn't long before she discovered something about Freda that she never knew: Freda was a psychic and read the tarot!

The very next day she knocked on Freda's door, while admiring the pentagram it was adorned with. Once inside she continued to gawp and stare at the house with Buddhas, pentagrams, a very busy altar and pictures she couldn't understand.

There was something here that called to her; she had butterflies going wild in her tummy but couldn't work out why. She had been for readings before so that wasn't it, was it just that this house felt so mysterious, but in a strange way welcoming?

The reading had started and Tabby sat quietly, not wanting to give anything away. Freda dealt the cards and looked at them deeply, being silent for what seemed like an eternity before she finally spoke. "You know you are a Psychic Medium, don't you?" Freda calmly asked and for a while her sentence hung in the air.

Really? A woman who did the school run, was training to be an Accountant and couldn't cook? Who walked the dog, wore sensible clothes and played at being a housewife? "Me? Really?" was all she could utter. When Freda asked her what she thought a Psychic looked like she couldn't help but look at the wild, exciting lady sat in front of her.

She was dressed from head to toe in black velvet with huge hooped earrings and gorgeous, tousled locks and Tabby couldn't help but think that her image epitomised the psychic of her imagination! As she looked again around the room the setting was perfect for Freda, everywhere she looked there were crystals and pentagrams…there was even a goat's head in the corner and light danced from the array of tea-lights that adorned the room.

Then Freda did something that changed Tabby's life forever – she dared her to find out for herself. As a teenager she could never resist a dare and it seemed the adult of today was also up for a challenge.

Before she could say 'ironing day' she had agreed to spend the next four Thursdays with Freda, to prove or disprove the theory of her abilities. She could never have imagined as she accepted Freda's offer that those four weeks would quite literally change her life.

The thought of spending time with Freda was both exciting and scary at the same time. She didn't tell her husband as she knew he would think it ridiculous. Anyway, what was there to tell? She thought she would be quite rubbish at any task she was set – she had a strong logical mind and was far too sensible to be a psychic!

On her first visit those thoughts quickly disappeared. The first exercise was Psychometry, which is reading the energy of an object to pick up information about its wearer.

As she sat with a man's gold wedding ring in her hand, she described the person's life down to the house they lived in, a description of their wife and children and the car they drove. Next she was asked to describe the dead person Freda was thinking of. After a minute of uncertainty she described their age, favourite t-shirt and way they left the planet, much to her disbelief!

So it appeared that Tabby really did live up to Freda's expectations. This was exciting, scary and also humbling to her to be able to connect with people and energy in this way, but Freda would say nothing and look on with a knowing smile. She wanted to ask endless questions about where all this information was coming from, but somehow she managed to keep quiet and would wait impatiently for the next week's session to arrive.

Each session Freda would challenge her with

something new and she would raise her eyebrows, knowing she couldn't do it. She would then be proved wrong as Freda guided her into trying everything at least once. Freda was a fantastic teacher, giving out pearls of wisdom in a humble way that expected no praise and gently pushed her to do more.

Tabby was a woman of words and would always have visualisations full of experiences to describe. Freda would give her opinion, but always encourage her to find her own explanation, or be ok with not knowing.

During their time spent together Freda calmly opened her eyes to a whole new world. It was as if a door had been unlocked showing her a crack of light; a way in to a new dimension.

It was here that patience was needed. Up until this point she had been searching for the missing part of herself, but years of working in a bank and logically getting on with life had left a healthy scepticism. How did this work? Why did it work? Where did the psychic muscle live? How was it that this gift had magically chosen her and why now? Freda just explained the facts; that everyone was a psychic, it was just that some people used their intuition more than others.

Gradually she learned a whole new vocabulary: visualisation, Psychometry, astral travelling, Mediumship, all the clairs – clairvoyance, clairaudience, clairsentience and two others that she could never remember!

She learned other new things too. She learned that up until this point she had never known what it was to truly relax. She learned that it was possible to communicate with your body, to heal a bit that hurt if you had the time. She learned to channel white light through her hands and send it to her children when they were unwell.

She learned to watch the world for signs that would guide her and to talk to the natural world around her. She would stop and smile as leaves danced without a breeze and say hello to the robin that stared intently at her through the window each morning – which was strange as he had never bothered to stop by before.

Through telling her mum of her experiences Tabby also learned of her history – apparently she had two great-grandmothers with similar talents. Her great-grandmother on her mum's side had read tea leaves and been the village midwife. Her great-grandmother on her dad's side had been a Medium and an amazing herbalist, curing her own son of his childhood illness with stinging nettle tea. All this history had been there, all the time waiting to be discovered; it was just that she had never thought to ask.

## TABBY TURNS THE TABLES

Once she had learned the basics it was time to practise some more. After the girls were dropped to the school gates with kisses, hugs and lunchboxes, she would hurry home, excited and on a mission. This was a stark contrast to her recent drifting.

The famous Casper would then be walked, dragging her across roads, through puddles and over soggy fields. Endlessly he would bound around sniffing and investigating with an energy that never ran out. He was nervous around other dogs, but he loved his walks with Tabby and would run circles around her, never going out of her view.

As always he would refuse to come back until she yelled, "Casper! Here!" in a voice that threatened no food or cuddles. Eventually he would sidle over to her with his head down and eyes full of shame and any frustration she had would melt away and be replaced with love for the pet that had stolen her heart.

Then it was time for the drag back home after which Casper would collapse into sleep. Finally, after what felt like a full day's work she would be free to engage in her new skills and practise, practise, practise!

Freda had taught her to visualise, which was like meditation but rather than not thinking you would create a journey to go on, perhaps deep into the roots of a tree or up in a hot air balloon.

While following the story you would see colours and receive gifts, each having a meaning. Tabby couldn't always work out what the meanings were, though some were quite obvious. The rest she would write down and share with Freda, who always seemed to explain them in a way that made sense.

Hours were spent on journey after journey, communing with spirits, guides and helpers. Aches and pains were relieved, chakras woken up and was it her imagination or was life a little more bearable? Over time her sense of purpose grew and she felt that each day her strength was returning. On days with Freda and in her own quiet time she felt an innate sense of calm and a real sense of inner power, as if something was awakening, though exactly what she didn't know.

Thursdays with Freda continued too, with new things to try every week. It was during one of these afternoons that another friendship was formed, but in a way she could never have imagined.

About a year before Tabby and Freda's fateful meeting, something strange happened that had seemed completely irrelevant at the time. Her beautiful blue-eyed daughter made an announcement: "I don't want to be called Lauren, Mum, call me Sanamaya." Lauren made it quite clear that this was a serious request by refusing point blank to be called anything else.

For three weeks this angelic looking cherub had quite happily gone along with life – as long as her newly acquired name was used. Then one day she calmly said, "You can call me Lauren again now." And so life went on.

This particular Thursday at Freda's, she was in the middle of a visualisation to connect with her spirit guide, which was a bit daunting really as she never realised that all this help was available to her. Freda explained that we all have a guide to watch over us on our life path, to steer us and help us when we need inspiration. What would her guide look like?

The next thing she knew she was having a conversation with a tall, muscular, bare chested American Indian with long, black plaited hair and buckskin trousers. "I am Shanamaya," he said in a booming yet playful voice.

Was it possible that her three-year-old had been in contact before her and one of them had misheard or mispronounced his name?

Shanamaya showed her where to go during her visualisations and would bow low bows as he gave her gifts and signs. Week after week he would be there as she journeyed, taking her to places to experience peace, showing her images when she asked questions and taking her hand in a way that made her feel completely safe and protected.

At that point she could not have imagined the significance of this meeting. She couldn't possibly have known that she had tapped into support, knowledge and guidance that would be there, twenty-four hours a day, throughout the horrific lows and the giggle-filled highs as her life unfolded.

***

So with Freda's help Tabby had opened a door. Where this journey would lead she had no idea. She knew she had only scratched the surface of what existed and that she was a complete beginner…and yet she felt as if this was more of a remembering than learning.

She learned more about her own reality too. She learned that her husband didn't mind this new 'hobby' of hers. If life didn't get interrupted and tea continued to appear, she could do as she wished. Her friends didn't quite get it, but that was ok too.

This was her gift; her secret world where she could go

and be understood. Where she could roam free and relax into a happiness all of her own. She had always felt as if she could be in a room of a thousand people and be quite alone, but during her afternoons and Thursday sessions she felt alive and herself, connected to an energy that was vibrant and pure, where she felt complete and understood. She knew that she was taking her first steps on a journey and that this time there was no rush to share.

It was during one of their last afternoons together that Freda quietly made a statement. "You know, everything you have learned is amazing, but remember one thing. You live in the real world, where you are supposed to learn, experience and grow. We can lose hours and days visualising, but part of our journey here on earth, as a human, is to make the changes necessary so we can enjoy every second of the life we have to live here, in the real everyday world."

The hardest decision of her life didn't even exist at this point, as she had a few more years of pain and medical attention to go through. One thing she did know though, was that while she loved her girls, her home, her dog and even her husband to some extent, she really didn't love her life.

She knew that a part of her was switched off and she

spent a large proportion of her life on automatic pilot. Her knowledge was expanding and her energy was returning, every day there were tiny signs that things were changing for the better, but still there was a sense that she was ignoring a very big lesson that was just around the corner.

It was at this point that she realised her magical journey may have to be put on hold for a while. This door had been opened and could never be closed again, but first her reality needed some attention. She was sure that her new guide would be here for her and that the Universe probably had a plan.

\*\*\*\*

# CHAPTER 4

The realisation that she was going to leave her husband happened on Christmas Eve.

Just like that, with no fanfare or flourish, Tabby made a calm decision as obvious as realising it would be Christmas Day tomorrow. Her husband's shouting had become a ritual in their household as it was his way of showing any frustration or getting his own way. This time it was the last straw, the final nail in the coffin.

They had been out for their Christmas Eve meal as was tradition, her in-laws always tried to meet up each year. There were adults and over-excited children squashed into a small space chattering away quite happily. There was the usual banter and jokes and the atmosphere was lovely.

Her husband's moods were quite unpredictable, so it

was no surprise when mediocre happiness turned to quiet sulking; this was something quite normal and all she could do was shrug her shoulders at her mother-in-law when she asked what the problem was.

What caused that final straw to snap was when her husband shouted at the girls, at point blank range and at full volume, for something their cousins had done. It was a surreal moment when she realised she wasn't going to shout. She wasn't even going to say anything.

As she cuddled the girls closely to her, dried their tears and tactfully changed the subject she realised that somewhere along the line she had forgotten how to fight.

Now that didn't really come as a great surprise to her when the events of the last few years were taken into account. The girls had been looked after, the tea made it on to the table most nights, but still her husband continued to swing between mildly happy and downright grumpy.

Despite her husband's negative view of the world, Tabby had initially retained her optimistic nature and happy disposition. Over the years, rather than argue, she had marvelled at how life changed and remained quite resolute that she could make everything better.

She had succeeded in getting her husband to change career and train in something he loved. She did however sigh quietly to herself when the moaning had started again within a couple of weeks.

She had juggled college herself and gone through eight years of accountancy training, while still earning the exact amount needed to pay that faithful mortgage. She had learned to bite her lip when she returned home exhausted from a night of numbers to start again, washing up and returning the house to order, sometimes even putting two sleepy angels to bed while their dad sat with the television on.

The studying had paid off though; while considering leaving she had a strange realisation. Rather than having to face the prospect of persuading a husband well versed at bullying and scaremongering to leave, she could simply move herself and her children.

That great new salary she now earned after years of number crunching would come in very handy she thought, as she flicked through the property pages and found a handful of houses near to school that she could afford. With that amazing and yet frightening realisation Tabby quietly put the paper down and went off to get the tea.

***

The first few months in their new house were a little

traumatic as you can imagine, with the girls taking some time to adjust to their new surroundings and the regime of sharing their time between parents. Tabby had done lots of guilt buying and there were lots of McDonald's outings and cinema trips, as well as the neighbours getting used to the smoke alarm going off as pizza after pizza got cremated.

The cottage that they had found was in a great location within walking distance of school and was quirky, which suited her quite nicely. They were tucked behind the village dairy and boasted beamed ceilings and thick, rustic walls.

There was an amazing Inglenook fireplace that she had adorned with lilies and the scent filled the house. The girls shared the largest bedroom with an en suite bathroom that they loved. Her own room was tiny and her futon bed very low and uncomfortable, yet she spent hours through the night tucked up in there with a pile of books.

It was during these hours alone at night that she had time to reflect back on the last few months. The journey that had brought her to where she was now seemed surreal, as if it had happened to someone else.

\*\*\*

The timing of her transition had been less than perfect.

Four months earlier just as she was studying for her final exams and on the same day as the Twin Towers of the World Trade Center collapsed, her nan had been diagnosed with an incurable cancer. Over the months the family had hidden their grief and busied themselves with her care and every day while studying Tabby made time to visit her nan in hospital.

When she had decided to leave her husband, her parents had enough on their plate. Her nan was frail, poorly and two operations had left her quite bewildered. The family decided that the best place for her was living with Tabby's mum and dad so she could get the twenty-four hour care she so desperately needed. Looking back it seemed fitting that she had chosen happiness at that time.

Her nan and granddad had enjoyed a blissful, contented marriage. They had been through a lot as a family, including losing their youngest child when he was just fourteen. They had stuck together through all the pain and supported each other.

Perhaps knowing she could never achieve this in her own marriage had spurred her on to make the move before her nan passed to spirit. Her illness had meant twenty-four hour a day care, so she spent a lot of time in her nan's company.

Tabby and her nan always shared a special bond, with a

shared sense of humour and an easy relationship. They had shared so many magical times together over the years that there was never a strained conversation and silences were easy. She would make sure her nan was dressed with her lipstick on, as appearances had always meant so much to her.

After her granddad died, her nan had been really lost, not having the partner who loved and supported her through the majority of her life. The girls being young meant lots of family outings and time to play, which turned the focus of the family onto them instead. This meant an even closer relationship and the bond between mother, daughter, granddaughter and great granddaughters had always been the envy of her friends.

She made the most of her precious time with her nan but kept her plans to herself. She had meticulously gone over the details of how and where, done all her thinking and mustered up all her courage. Tabby had recently purchased a new car and gradually over time she had packed a bag and added their passports. The night before she was leaving, while her mum raided the freezer for peas, she rather calmly shared the news that she was leaving the next day.

***

## TABBY TURNS THE TABLES

Tabby adopted a great routine when the girls visited their dad, spending the weekend roaming like a gypsy from friend to friend. She liked the reputation she had earned as a party animal, preferring this to admitting the truth that she was scared of her own company.

Since her teens she had always been part of a crowd but now she was an independent, single woman. People around her seemed jealous, but to her this alien world filled her with dread – when she had time to fill, panic would set in until a last minute trip out was hurriedly conjured up.

The upside of single life hadn't gone unnoticed though, like crisp eating while reading in bed. She now stayed up late and rose early which was a complete shift in routine. There were spontaneous shopping trips to buy paraphernalia on a whim and their house that initially had been stark was gradually being filled up. There were an endless string of Tupperware and Body Shop parties where her friends gathered and this was all great fun.

There were always friends and family visiting or outings to be had; it turned out Liza was a dab hand at map reading at the tender age of eleven, so they would all pile into the car and head off on adventures. She had never strayed far from her home town and yet now there was no stopping them.

## TABBY TURNS THE TABLES

They had recently found their way to Exeter and a McFly concert; the three of them dancing and giggling the night away and then sleepily sharing the journey home.

There was quite a bit to deal with of late with the now suitably named ex-husband. Initially she had thought it would all work out ok, as she had left without needing to take any furniture. This had partly been done out of fear but was also deliberate, as the girls still shared their dad's house often. She would hate them to go back to an empty space and she genuinely didn't want to hurt anyone.

The children had been exceptionally grown up and decided to split their time equally between parents, so the childcare arrangements had been easy to agree upon. Extra clothes were bought and she found to her surprise that she could be organised when she needed to be!

Apparently though, it was inconceivable for her ex-husband to think that she had just 'had enough'. There were a few interesting conversations that she couldn't avoid when the blame went from an affair to the early onset of the menopause. When deciding to leave, she thought that her husband would be relieved when she admitted what neither of them could acknowledge before; that the love had gone and they were very different people now.

But it seemed that her ex-husband didn't share her opinion. He spent hours following her car, begging with her parents to order her back home and turning up early in the morning so that the girls would let him in. She had tried to be reasonable, allowing conversations and calmly carrying on with her life. It was hard not to scream when she opened her eyes to see him towering over her, but somehow she managed. This was the girls' father after all and she didn't want them to be scared.

Once her ex-husband realised she wasn't going back, however, he became more threatening. There had been late night phone calls telling her in detail what would happen if ever she denied him access to his children. Despite her efforts to keep up some interaction for the sake of her children, Tabby finally admitted defeat.

The last episode and the final straw had occurred on Father's Day outside their house. There had been much shouting from her ex-husband and any attempts she made to calm him down seemed to inflame the situation. Finally, the scenario that felt like a scene from a horrific movie resulted in her life being threatened, physically, in front of her girls. She had backed away helplessly, leaving her shocked, pale-faced children with their father as he drove away at high speed.

## TABBY TURNS THE TABLES

In shock, she rushed back into her house and while shaking like a leaf, consulted the police. Thankfully the girls were returned home after a couple of hours, being watched carefully by neighbours. The solicitors had been called in and a few boundaries were put in place. She thought her heart would break as she watched her two angels crossing a no-man's land between their cars during their frequent trips to and fro.

On top of this upset and heartbreak, she had another wrench to deal with. Casper up until this point had been living with her ex-husband as she rented their temporary home. This had been nice for the girls as they had Casper to play with when they stayed with their dad. Now though, he decided that he could no longer keep the family pet and found him a home with family that lived in Scotland.

Agonising over it she realised that she had no real choice. Even when she did buy her own house she would still be working full time. She knew in her heart that a house by a loch in Scotland with a loving family was the right choice, not the easy choice.

She had been so brave over recent months, but this last piece of news was too much. There were several days where she sat alone in her office, crunching numbers and defeating spreadsheets, with tears rolling silently down her face.

Being scared and having situations without a magic answer were all new to Tabby. She realised that she had lived her whole life within very safe limits…until now.

As a child there had always been friends or family around her and her working life involved lots of people. Whenever there was something she had to do that involved being alone, her mum had volunteered to come along too.

When she still lived at home she had attended a training course in Cardiff. To get the train would have been easy, but her mum and dad decided on a shopping trip that day. They escorted her to the course venue first, shopped for the day, then collected her and shared the journey home.

It was fantastic having parents that cared for her, but was it possible to care too much? This was the first time in her life that her parents couldn't save her…or was it just the simple fact that Tabby decided to take care of herself?

Although scared, she found an inner strength that she never knew existed. When her ex-husband shouted she found herself staying calm. If she had to ring or speak to him initially she would delay the call and shake for two days solid before plucking up the courage to do it.

Try as she might she couldn't stop this, until one day she found some additional bravery. She told her ex-husband that she would only speak to him if he didn't shout or swear. It took putting the phone down numerous times that day, but after that they could hold a calm conversation, something that she had thought impossible...and the shaking stopped.

Her daughters continued to amaze her as they coped with their parents' emotions. Initially they asked why they needed to live in two places, but the events of recent months had seamlessly turned them into diplomats, choosing to be economical with the minutiae of their lives and only sharing the details that wouldn't initiate another string of phone calls.

This showed her a glimpse of the amazing adults her children would become. There had been so many proud mummy moments as the girls gained confidence and learned new skills. They could both express themselves and tell a tale or two and often had the adults around them captivated.

Her children really thrived in grown up company, with happy times spent with family and friends on days out. Various role models were appearing during this time and it warmed her heart seeing so many people around her making time to educate, guide and entertain her children!

Initially Liza was furious with her mum for leaving and she could understand why. Liza wanted answers and reasons to satisfy her enquiring nature and she couldn't give her a real, concrete reason why she was leaving. How could she? It would be impossible to point out all their dad's faults to her children, then still expect them to love him.

Tabby didn't want this to turn into a point scoring exercise either; she had seen many divorces that had. Initially they had talked over telling the children and come up with the story that they loved the girls very much, but didn't love each other. When the time came to sit the girls down though, her ex-husband simply said, "Mummy has decided to leave and take you away as she doesn't love Daddy anymore."

This instant and perhaps Freudian slip effortlessly put the blame at her door. At that point though, she hadn't cared how it was done, just that she wanted it over with as quickly as possible. She wanted to move the girls, get them settled and try to keep some form of normality going.

The first few months were a see-saw of over-compensating one minute and coping with the backlash the next. Lauren had always been an easy-going child and was too young to be the victim of mind games. She went from parent to parent with a smile on her face and rarely got upset. Liza was older though and always needed to know the details.

Maybe she realised her mum wasn't telling the truth or the whole story and wanted to understand. After weekends with her dad she would come back on a mission to cause chaos and bad feeling and this was really hard to cope with, as she could see the hurt and confusion in those huge brown eyes.

Mostly Tabby gave in and soothed the situation by pandering to every whim. The guilt was huge, how could you give your daughters a reason big enough for them to accept living apart from their dad?

Over time, she knew that she had to give her children some boundaries and so quietly got more and more assertive, gradually insisting on a few more rules and occasionally putting her foot down.

It was on one such occasion that she gave her daughters 'the look', something her own dad had always used to instantly make her blood run cold when she was misbehaving. She realised that throughout her daughters' lives she had always been undermined and ignored. She wondered why she had never noticed before.

## TABBY TURNS THE TABLES

After the Father's Day 'incident' where her daughters had clearly seen the temper and anger of their dad, Liza's attitude changed. Suddenly the bubble she had been trying to keep up around her children had burst and there was no hiding the facts any more.

The truth was out and it was a relief after all this time to drop the pretence. The bond that had always been there between Tabby and her beautiful daughters just continued to intensify from this point, which made her heart sing.

There were more cuddles and giggles and day by day she watched as they all started healing their wounds and relaxing into their new life together.

\*\*\*\*

## CHAPTER 5

Tabby led a double life.

On the outside, nothing had really changed except for her hair colour. Having never been 'allowed' to dye her hair, her new found freedom meant a myriad of colours had been trialled recently, from a sneaky plum to the outrageous pink with blonde streaks. It was true her boss had commented that the hair didn't really befit a company accountant, but it was said with a hint of sarcasm and affection so was suitably ignored.

She could now get out of bed without grumbling or snoozing the alarm multiple times. She could get them all out of the house with appropriate school bags, gym kits and lunches – although there was the occasional slip up which she considered a human moment!

There had been a few liberating moments, like finally

admitting her absolute revulsion for cake baking. Amazingly she discovered that both of her daughters had a passion for baking, so hours were then spent with packet mixes and lots of hundreds and thousands. Colourful creations were made at a moment's notice and all future school requests for cakes were met with a swift trip to the supermarket and hours of supervised fun and giggles.

On the inside though, that was a different story!

By day she was the sensible working single mum and Accountant with an organised focus, immaculate clothes and spectacles on her nose. By night and on child free weekends her real self emerged. Hours were spent immersed in books – from pagan ways to angel inspirations, from Taoism to chakras, aura sensing and tarot.

There was so much out there to find out about, she couldn't read fast enough to quench her thirst for knowledge. She experimented with new ideas and practised more visualisations. She had scraps of paper scattered all around the house with poignant phrases, spells and meditations all saved for the moments when they would come in handy.

She realised her possibilities were endless and she wondered how she had missed this fact growing up. She always felt that she was missing pieces of the jigsaw and now it seemed that she had found them. She was free to do as she pleased and she knew what she didn't want, but what did she want?

She knew that the disciplines in all these books made people happy and could see elements that would work for her, but none of them fitted her perfectly so did that mean they were wrong for her?

There were other changes too.

She had always hated winter and tucked up with big baggy jumpers and cups of tea as soon as it got dark. Her depression and gloom would draw in with the nights and only after her birthday in February would she start to resume evening outings.

After reading a pagan book called 'A Witch Alone' by Marian Green everything changed. She felt elation and illumination, as if a light had been turned on in her life and she remembered a part of herself that she had lost. Eagerly she turned page after page, totally spellbound by the contents of this book.

Through learning about the seasons she understood the cycle of life. Spring time was for planting seeds, for nurturing new dreams and making plans. Summer was a time of fruition and celebration where plans became reality. Autumn was for giving thanks, then clearing out anything that was no longer working to make space.

Winter was all about looking after yourself, letting go of old habits and resting ready for the next cycle of life to begin. Generations before us had naturally followed these cycles, but all our technology and fast living had meant that we had lost our way, it seemed.

She pored over and embraced her new knowledge and watched as she started to change.

She now enjoyed bracing walks on sunny winter days and would collect leaves and pebbles on the way. Every drive became a pleasure as she took in her surroundings and appreciated nature's beauty. Each change in season, blooming flower and animal were noticed and smiled at.

One particularly rainy day on the way to school in the car she screeched to a halt as she spotted a fallen branch that would be perfect as a staff for rituals. She pleaded with Liza to jump out and grab it despite her protestations. As a drenched and squealing Liza jumped back in the car and wedged the branch beneath their feet, she thought the girls quite liked her new unpredictability and they giggled their way to school.

She also read more about the moon and its cycles and realised that she had always had this affinity with moon energy. She had spent hours in her unhappy times watching the moon and the shadows it threw over the gardens below. She had always used new moon energy for creative projects and a waning moon for bringing in changes, she just hadn't known it.

So did this mean she was a witch? She really wasn't sure. There was a part of her that quite liked the idea, but how would she explain her journey to her friends? Could she put into words all that had happened and the depth of feeling that she experienced?

She decided there should be much more discovery and experimentation before mentioning it to her mother.

In a lot of the books she had read, she had been fascinated with the elements. Being a Piscean meant she had a real connection to water and loved being near the sea. This connection also meant bursting into tears at the drop of a hat. Any sad film would reduce her to tears, even a crying child in a supermarket would start her eyes prickling!

This high emotion had disappeared during the illnesses and stresses of her tricky years, when she could withstand any amount of trauma without so much as a lump in the throat. After her illness, the return to normal had included lots of wailing as her emotions found their balance again. Her 'piece de resistance' had been bursting into tears and begging her mum not to go away for the weekend, something she was now not particularly proud of but put down to the healing process.

She had always been a sympathetic person, to a fault, so one day decided to redress the balance. Life could be hard and stressful when you were a working single parent and she craved a little sympathy and understanding herself. She had read a lot about spells and understood the basics. She decided that if she really was a witch she should work with some spells and get to know the elements.

She read lots of books about ritual and hatched a plan. After lengthy preparations which included salt baths and meditation, she performed her first ritual. She felt great as she turned to the West, called in the element of water and asked for others to give her sympathy and help her more.

It was during the next day that she realised she must have mixed up her words. She had volunteered to help out on the school trip, got collared to do extra reading duty, bought a Big Issue and dropped her daughter's friend's home before noticing there could be a problem.

Instead of being helped she had doubled up the helping – how could that be? That wasn't all. A few days later she stumbled into the lounge to feed the fish, only to discover them flipping all over the floor! The seventeen gallon fish tank had cracked, so operation 'Save the Fishies' had then ensued, involving lots of bowls, a water heater and an over-used Vax.

That wasn't all. Three days after that the washing machine flooded. She wasn't sure who was more embarrassed as the engineer held up a bra wire as the culprit. Her cheeks burned and she was very sure of who was more embarrassed the following week when a 20p did the same thing.

Unperturbed she went about discovering the element of fire…

This wasn't quite as dramatic – the iron, the microwave, the toaster and several light bulbs were the only casualties. At this point on her journey though she thought she would have a rest from getting to know the elements…even if it was just for the simple reason that she couldn't afford to replace any more appliances!

The rituals felt amazing. She felt a connection with the Universe; she felt relaxed, peaceful, happy and safe. Ritual seemed to come naturally to her and she seemed to instinctively know what colours to use, how many candles to have and how to decorate her cauldron. She loved creating her sacred space and communing with God and Goddess, her words seeming to come from somewhere poetic deep within. She would sit patiently as the messages flowed. It was clearly just the expression of her intentions that needed work.

Now the world was becoming a bigger place too. She had once thought of her home town as the centre of her world and a trip to the neighbouring city involved a technical plan with lots of preparation. Gradually though, she had mastered map reading (nearly) and then invested in a satnav, so more adventures ensued.

It amazed her friends that although she could now drive to London she would still get lost coming out of the pub toilets, but she reminded them of the Piscean symbol: two fish, swimming in opposite directions!

The thought of being lost used to scare her rigid, as if the world would stop spinning if you didn't know where you were. This was daft really she thought, as you are usually only a street or two away from where you need to be. She was quite pleased to be getting rid of the control freak inside, who she hadn't known existed in the first place!

## TABBY TURNS THE TABLES

So where does a newly liberated hippy go in the summer? Glastonbury Festival of course! She and her friend Terri decided to go for it, imagining balmy afternoons sat in the sunshine, glasses of wine, great music and the freedom to explore, what could be better? Together they dreamed of wandering the stalls and exploring by day and dancing their feet off by night – the whole thing sounded amazing!

She had never camped before, preferring holidays in hotels with swimming pools and room service. It would be a great adventure to sleep under the stars and be close to nature. She thought planning would be the key and prepared for every eventuality with torches, wellies, washing up bowls and fresh fruit. Unsure of what a festival goer wears she packed an array of t-shirts, jumpers, jeans and shorts as well as her newly bought sparkly flip flops.

On the day she was so excited, the car was packed to the gunnels but she had never been a good judge of space and the thought that she would need to carry this lot had never entered her head.

The girls had spent the evening before sharing several glasses of wine, so their heads were a little sore too, but this was outweighed by their enthusiasm. It was only after the three mile, sweat covered, life-threatening trudge from car to camping spot that common sense reappeared: did they really need the washing up bowl, clothes line, cans of Pimms and all those spare shoes?

Once settled though the weekend was everything she had hoped for, with amazing music, sun-filled afternoons and so much laughter. She felt as if she was living her youth for the very first time, as if she had been old before her time and had been given a chance to discover the bits she had missed the first time around. On the second day they wandered a bit further and discovered her Mecca: The Healing Field. In this corner of heaven tucked away from the music she discovered by chance a feeling she remembered: complete peace.

It was in this cattle field temporarily transformed by ribbons, tipis, music and tie-dye that Tabby remembered her Thursday sessions with Freda and her thoughts became clearer. It had always felt as if there was a connection to a faith or energy that would have given her support, but she had never quite felt completely tuned in. Over the last few years she had found little time for anything that wasn't coping with one or other of life's demands – until now!

Every spare minute between her favourite bands was spent in this field. Tarot readings were had, healing was received and there were hours spent lying in the grass watching the clouds. In this state she could literally feel all her worries ebbing away, all the stress leaving her body and there were a few light bulb moments where she understood pieces of her life too. There were tears, there were giggles and there was dancing too. It was safe to say that she had truly found her bliss and she wanted so much more of it!

Glastonbury finished soon enough, much to their dismay. It was quite strange one moment being a free spirit with bare feet and a smile and the next being back behind a desk in an office. It seemed life was intent on showing itself as a scale, sliding from one end to the other on a daily basis.

One minute she was mother; the next a working professional. Daytimes being responsible; evenings foot loose and fancy free. One minute she would be giggling with her girls and painting each others' toenails, the next she would need to be the stern yet gentle disciplinarian. A moment of stress was balanced by hours full of bliss.

She now found herself saying yes to any new experience; she would try everything once and see how she felt. Years had been spent indoors letting life pass by, but this wouldn't happen anymore.

If there was somewhere to go, by herself or with the girls, she was up for it. If the sun was shining they would be somewhere with a picnic and usually a group of friends. Every day was a chance for adventure and she didn't want to miss anything.

The whole rollercoaster of life started out as exhausting, but after a while it became amusing to her. There was also a realisation that nothing, nothing at all, was permanent. While looking out of the window one day she looked at the trees and grass, everything was moving.

Birds flew, bees buzzed and the grass danced, nature was alive and constantly changing. It had seemed like security to have lived a life where you knew what was going to happen. It felt safe when life was predictable, even when that meant an argument or a moment of giving in, but was it really?

Was security accepting the status quo, going along with your life because this was what you knew even if it made you unhappy? Or was security something you grew yourself by knowing that you would cope with whatever life threw at you?

She realised that her unhappiness had led to doubting herself and losing her energy, which made her world smaller and restrictive rather than secure. The smaller her world got the smaller she felt, any self-confidence or sparkle ebbed away over time.

It had taken a huge amount of energy and resolve to

make her recent changes and there had been times when she felt she would be swept away by the rollercoaster as it had swooped to its lowest depths. So many times she faced challenges or had no idea what to do next.

The reward for all this had been a genuine, long-lasting security and a belief in herself, along with a deepened relationship with her children and some genuine, loving friends. The latter was priceless and she was deeply thankful for her journey.

\*\*\*\*

## CHAPTER 6

It was at this point that Tabby discovered a new passion.

Her life had introduced her to holistic therapy years earlier after her debilitating headache and her recent days spent in the healing field had inspired her to discover more.

She knew that the body talked, sending out messages about what it needed help with and that relief and sometimes a cure can be found without popping a single pill. By reading books and talking to people, she had learned that there were so many therapies! If she was going to choose one to learn which would it be? How did you learn? How did you know if you would be good at it?

So again, the Universe gave her a hand.

On holiday, sitting by the pool, she made a new friend.

## TABBY TURNS THE TABLES

The lady on the next sun bed also had two children and this was her first holiday on her own with them.

She had arrived a few days earlier with the girls, so helped Sue out a little, telling her the times of the various kiddie activities and the location of the pharmacy. Their children instantly made friends and spent hours splashing and laughing, leaving the two mums to chat.

They got on really well and Sue even knew the writer of her favourite book, a coincidence that hadn't gone unnoticed to the newly tuned in Tabby!

A few conversations later Sue told her she was a Reiki Master. She had never heard of Reiki and didn't quite know what it was or how it worked.

As Sue explained all the details, it seemed that it was quite similar to the white light healing she had used when her girls were poorly, except you needed an attunement and to work through the three levels.

Sue ran her own Holistic Therapy centre, where different therapists could practise. Each day Sue would add more details and explain more about her world, which seemed mysterious, fun and amazing. Sue reminded her of Freda in many ways and there was a kindness in her eyes.

So as their holiday came to an end, Tabby returned with a great tan, a relaxed body and a desire to learn Reiki! She thought that a master would literally pop up, but couldn't hide her disappointment when a chance meeting didn't materialise. "Oh well," thought Tabby, "when the time is right."

Wherever she went though there were signs for Reiki practitioners, from seaside trips to adverts in papers all she would read was Reiki, Reiki, and Reiki.

A few months later she was having coffee and catching up with a friend who had recently met a new man. He sounded perfect; kind, loving, an artist and into spirituality. Imagine the look on her face when, in the middle of the conversation her friend casually added, "Oh did I say, Jonathan is a Reiki Master."

That was the synchronicity she had been waiting for. Within a matter of weeks she and Mary received their Reiki One attunement. The experience was full of more signs from the Universe that she was exactly where she was meant to be.

During the meditation she felt an eye in the middle of her forehead spring open – it looked to her like an Egyptian eye. Was this her third eye? She wasn't sure.

As she sat with her eyes closed a beautiful violet light danced before her eyes and she felt an overwhelming peace and calm that was completely new. Emotions flooded through her with an intensity that she had never experienced before. Her whole body tingled and she could feel every cell. She felt as if the day had gone on for an eternity and she floated home, filled with a new purpose and wondering at the magical world around her.

Tabby's holistic journey had started.

She loved the way Reiki started to change how she viewed the world. She seemed to have more patience and rather than catch the bugs her children brought home from school she would only sniffle for a couple of days.

She couldn't wait to know more and learned Indian Head Massage and Reflexology too. Growing up she had never been a hands-on person and would freeze if anyone except her family tried to hug her. Now though she discovered she didn't mind bodies!

She learned how responsive the body can be when given the space and time. Of course there is never any promise to cure anything, as everyone has their own journey to follow, but our bodies are quite good at healing themselves.

She practised her new skills on the girls and her friends – anyone who mentioned an ache got the offer of a treatment, something that proved very popular! She seemed to work with people on an instinctive level, using her new intuition to feel where her hands needed to go and connecting with her guides to ask that everything happened for the highest good.

Reflexology required more study and initially the anatomy and physiology was hard as she had shied away from any form of science at school, particularly biology! It was amazing now though, how hard she could work with her new found purpose.

Learning how the systems of the body worked together was fascinating. The practical treatments seemed to flow effortlessly and she would disappear into a world of healing and calm.

All the while, she met more friends with a similar view on life. On every course there were new connections and so many synchronicities. She realised that everyone had their own story or journey that got them to learn about the holistic world.

It warmed her heart to hear how these people had overcome their own challenges, which were usually very painful and traumatic. Every one of them had come through their experiences stronger, more in tune with themselves and with a yearning to help other people.

As soon as she was able she learned Reiki Two with Jonathan and was overjoyed when she could add this therapy to her practise. There were so many ways that

## TABBY TURNS THE TABLES

Reiki could help a person and they didn't even have to be with you! This skill proved useful when she received texts from her girls when they were poorly and away from home.

Reiki Two brought with it another bonus – she quit smoking in a rather dramatic way. She had only ever smoked socially, usually after a glass of wine or two and would never feel the urge to smoke the following day, much to the annoyance of her addicted friends.

The evening after Reiki Two she decided to go out for a few drinks and a nice chilled out evening. Imagine her surprise then when her first cigarette sent her running to the toilet to be sick! There was a further evening of 'trying' which had the same result, after which Tabby concluded she was indeed a non-smoker and had Reiki energy to thank for it!

Her eyes had been opened further to the amazing benefits of holistic therapy and she was much more self-assured, but she still had so much more to learn and experience.

A phrase stuck in her mind: "Healer heal thyself." She had read that to keep your own energy in balance and to be the best therapist you could possibly be you needed to stay healthy and address any past traumas that may affect you today.

## TABBY TURNS THE TABLES

So she and her friend Charlotte decided to take a road trip to Glastonbury. They booked into an amazing place, each room having a theme and theirs was the Orient. Beautiful silk hangings adorned every wall and each table carried ornaments and symbolism. Looking around she marvelled at the peace she felt here, the B&B was nestled beneath Glastonbury Tor and she instantly felt safe.

Tabby had been with her husband since her teens and had never been away with friends, so it was exciting and new to be experiencing a girly weekend.

For hours they didn't stop talking and explored the rest of the house, with its tranquil gardens and meditation spaces.

Glastonbury was an amazing place to be. A walk up the Tor took every breath she had, but the view at the top was worth it. Standing at the top she felt an energy coursing through her, as if the earth had a heartbeat that connected directly to this magical place and in turn to her.

She could have stayed here for hours and Charlotte was quite happy to share the moment. They sat on the grass and talked at length about life, the Universe and everything!

While exploring the High Street she realised that here you could be anyone and wear anything; no one would notice you. In her own life, although she was changing so much, she still cared about what people thought.

Every other shop had tarot cards, crystals, goddesses and witty bumper stickers. "My other car is a broom" particularly appealed to her, but she didn't think her mum would cope if she turned up sporting that one, or her boss for that matter! The people here were very different from the shoppers in Bath. No one seemed hurried and most people were smiling.

There was a holiday atmosphere that wasn't just coming from the tourists, everyone seemed at peace and Tabby loved it.

She decided she wanted a treatment while she was here, but as usual her individuality demanded attention so she searched in shop after shop, looking for something really alternative. Near the top of the High Street, standing in a doorway was a man with an amazing smile. His name was Juan and he was from Peru. He had only been in Glastonbury for two weeks so was offering taster treatments.

Thai massage sounded fun and she found herself swept along by his disarming smile and obvious enthusiasm for his chosen therapy. Before she could stop and ask what was involved or check what Charlotte thought, her enthusiasm had her being led up the stairs.

# TABBY TURNS THE TABLES

On surveying the room her enthusiasm melted away with her bravery and she could feel the hairs stand up on the back of her neck. On the floor there was an old, faded, red velvet curtain – and nothing else. Realising she was going to need to lay on this she also remembered she was wearing her floaty, romantic skirt and hoped she had remembered to put on really big pants!

Juan asked her to relax, but relaxed was not how she felt! She checked in with Shanamaya as she frequently did these days, only to see a smirking spirit guide with his arms crossed saying, "You asked for different…"

So for a full forty-five minutes her limbs were tugged, stretched and manipulated into positions she never realised her body was capable of.

Juan had very strong thumbs she realised, as every muscle and sinew got a complete workout. Some of the movements were quite relaxing, others positively painful, but Juan was indeed an expert at his trade and was very enthusiastic throughout.

Sitting with her legs crossed facing the window she thought the session should nearly be over, as every muscle had been put through its paces. What happened next though took her completely by surprise…

Expertly grabbing her under the arms, Juan planted his feet firmly behind her bottom and before she could shriek he rolled backwards, jettisoning Tabby into the air. It was here, suspended above Juan's obviously muscular body she realised why Shanamaya had been smirking, as Juan shouted, "Fly Tabby, fly, you are as free as a bird!"

In a rather subdued fashion she quickly paid for her taster and got most of the way down the street before Charlotte could get her to share her experience. Charlotte then had to buy cake as penance for laughing so much. After an hour or so when the shock had subsided though, she realised that she felt bloody fantastic!

\*\*\*

So now she had a trail of qualifications to her name and insurance, but was unsure what to do next.

She daydreamed of how fabulous it would be if her accountant job was three days a week so she could work part-time as a therapist. She had learned from past experience that things had a way of working out, so she did what she'd phrased "Giving it up to the Universe."

Sure enough within a couple of months her job had extra tasks added to it, meaning she would need to work ten days a week to keep up. Even her reluctant boss had to admit that she wasn't capable of pulling that off, so she retained the senior tasks and gave the rest away to her newly appointed assistant. This new routine saved the company a few thousand pounds…and left her excited and working three days a week, marvelling at the wonders of the Universe!

The next year or so was spent working in a variety of therapy rooms and she was able to put her new skills into practise, both as a therapist but also as a marketer. Tabby found leaflet design and wording for websites quite enjoyable. She was quite comfortable coping with the stressful three days accounting and then four days split between looking after the girls and giving therapies.

She continued to use Reiki on herself every day and gradually she noticed changes to her health and energy. She found herself craving fruit and vegetables and it appeared that her temper had calmed itself.

In the past she rarely had angry outbursts but when she did they were loud and caused quite a stir in the house. As soon as she shouted, she would instantly regret the atmosphere that followed. As Reiki worked its magic she found herself much more calm and able to talk things through.

As a family the three of them had settled into a great routine. With the girls growing up it felt more like she was sharing a house with her friends than being the parent. The house was often filled with laughter as they all liked similar programmes on TV, or to dance to their favourite music. Their house was often full of other children too, it seemed the girls' friends liked to be around this newly relaxed and happy parent!

Sometimes she felt torn away from her family by her responsibility of being a single parent. Her job meant she had to work from 9am until 5pm and so she missed class assemblies and the odd parents evening when she worked late. At these times she envied the mums that were always there for their children, but reminded herself of the coffee mornings in the past where the mums would moan about their husbands or being bored.

Her mum had always been there for her girls as her nan had been there for her. She would know exactly what to do with them and gave them all the cuddles and attention they needed.

When she arrived to collect the girls, the whole house would be disrupted with toys, crafts and games strewn around to keep them entertained. Sometimes there was cooking, or pom pom making and there would always be stories to be told and giggles to be had. It was a huge comfort to know that her mum was on hand and so lovely to her grandchildren, but still she wanted to be there.

## TABBY TURNS THE TABLES

Lauren was often misunderstood both by children and teachers alike and it pained her that she couldn't be by her side – preferably twenty-four hours a day – but at least to be a smiling face at the school gate after a stressful day. Lauren never complained though and her big sister's protective nature came in handy as she would keep a watchful eye and ask her friends to look out for Lauren too.

Her job, even though stressful and quite often panic-filled, provided a security blanket, something that she assured herself was needed. So was it her imagination or was the Universe trying to get her to make more changes? Why else did her boss become more bullying, his demands more impossible and his taunts more cruel?

Initially she and her boss had enjoyed a cheeky, sarcastic relationship and she always quipped back with a smile and something witty. Perhaps her boss thought that she had a thick skin; her past meant that she didn't.

Over time witty sarcasm turned to cutting remarks and jibes when her children were poorly and she had to stay home. There were frequent reminders of how rubbish she was at her job where once there had been praise. Any upcoming deadlines were highlighted by sarcastic e-mails calling her a hippy.

One day sitting at her desk she noticed that she could

clearly hear her own heartbeat, going way too fast and thumping in her chest. Her pulse was racing and there were beads of sweat on her forehead. She knew for certain that if she kept up this level of stress her health would suffer. She realised that her time to move on had come. Again she turned her gaze skywards and asked for some divine intervention.

Strangely it wasn't a divine act that caused the end of her employment, but a nasty, sarcastic text on Christmas Eve that finally made her snap. She took a deep breath, made up several witty comebacks in her head and plotted a few forms of revenge…and then calmly replied that she was done and would rather stack shelves in Asda than go back after Christmas.

\*\*\*\*

## CHAPTER 7

Tabby was a fully fledged, self-employed person.

She had a website and some very pretty leaflets, an insurance certificate and a smart uniform. She also had some customers who she saw at home or at the treatment room she rented nearby. She was full of inspiration and ideas for her new business and seemed to always be smiling these days.

She had introduced the tarot to her business and enjoyed her work. There were a few people who wanted her to make decisions for them; should they leave their boyfriend or get another job? It was hard sometimes explaining that free will is at work here and only they can choose the right path for them, but mostly her clients were happy with her readings.

She sometimes wondered where her inspiration came

from, but trusted that she was getting the information for a reason. Her readings were always well received and she was lucky that her clients kept in touch and told her how helpful the readings had been.

She now worked with Shanamaya at her side and never questioned his guidance, he always seemed to know what to add to a reading to make it that much clearer.

Sometimes it was an image that appeared in her mind, other times it was a phrase. If there was an illness the person was suffering with, she would get a milder version of their symptoms and pain, just long enough to get recognition. It made her laugh to think of the number of conditions she had experienced while working with people!

She enjoyed the freedom self-employment gave her. She had coffee mornings with friends, days on the sofa when her children were poorly and a general feeling of being in charge of her own destiny. After a while though it dawned on her that mostly what she had was a very enjoyable hobby that wouldn't pay her mortgage! Unperturbed by this false start, she went on to get more organised and her company was truly born.

It was here that her social approach to life kicked in. Working with people giving one-to-one readings and therapies was great and Tabby loved seeing people change before her eyes. The change she had seen in her own life made her think: there were a lot of people on this planet that had no idea that an alternative to stress existed.

How many people were there working in offices, popping pills for this and that and accepting it as normal? What if she could arrange events that would be fun to go to and not too weird, so even a complete beginner could turn up and feel welcome?

Events with a Twist were invented! From summer garden parties, to psychic suppers and the Love Life! Roadshow™, event after event was arranged, planned, worked for and actioned.

Sometimes people came in their hoards, other times her events were 'a little quiet'. Unperturbed, her positive approach and glass full to overflowing nature shone through on even the quietest of days. She was in her element and on a mission, always dreaming up more events and working on new ideas.

Unknowingly and inspired by her passion, she had turned into an evangelist, going on the radio, writing for magazines and talking to anyone that would listen about the choices we have in life and how changes can be subtle and tiny and really make a difference.

It made her laugh when she now spoke in public without a second thought. There was a time when speaking up at a meeting of three people would have her meticulously preparing her words and sweating in apprehension. It also fascinated her that she had been invited onto the radio in the first place!

As Tabby created a need, the Universe provided the solution. So many conversations started with, "Wouldn't it be amazing if…" and then a few weeks later she would realise that it had happened!

Having her own business was a real adventure. Working with people came naturally, but what about all the behind the scenes stuff?

When you worked in a large company there was always someone else to do your admin, sort out the insurance, sell the products and do the marketing…she had always just looked after the numbers, preparing spreadsheets, reports and budgets. "Spreadsheets are sexy," she had always joked when her boss was wading through her endless numbers.

Her new company also meant her legendary stationary fetish could come to the fore – hours were spent perusing the latest catalogue and deciding how to colour co-ordinate her office. Gradually she picked up the basics of the bits she didn't know about. Coming up with a new slogan or event name was always easy, she had been a bit of a writer and poet when she was younger so playing with words just happened.

Tabby felt that she was guided to the names she chose, sometimes seeing an image of a smug looking American Indian with his arms crossed and a smile on his face!

Selling her services was a bit tricky though – how do you tell people why they should come to your event without sounding big-headed? What she lacked in business acumen though she made up for with enthusiasm.

Some people she worked with nicknamed her 'The Puppy' and she could see why, bounding around rallying anyone who would listen with exclamations of how brilliant it would all be and the fun they would have.

She found there was a pattern to her work: if she ran out of energy one week, the next week would be quiet. Again the phrase 'healer heal thyself' came in and she found she had to balance time with people and time spent alone.

When she had worked in a job the money was there at the end of the month, being self-employed meant that funds were a little disjointed. Life was a journey of feast and famine, quite challenging when your mortgage arrives on the same day regardless!

It did seem that she was getting help though. If there was something that she needed, an opportunity to earn money would present itself. When she needed a new therapy bed at a cost of £180 she sighed, knowing it would have to wait.

She found that she couldn't resist a smile though when a few days later she was offered a corporate event in Cardiff that would pay £180. The money didn't land in her lap; she always had to work for it in some way or another.

Sometimes she would meet people that declared they didn't have to work as "The Universe would provide for them."

This was all well and good, she thought, if you lived on a mountain top and ate berries!

Tabby couldn't help but giggle when she noticed these people didn't do that – they had top of the range mobile phones and nice cars but would still plead poverty – the Universe really had a job on its hands trying to provide for everyone.

On one occasion when she was panicking about her finances, she decided to take action. She had met a business coach called Paul who ran some local networking events and he had always spent time chatting to her. She decided that she needed some help with her business, that she couldn't pull it off by herself and at this rate she would be back working as an Accountant soon.

Paul had given her some homework. She had to score all the elements of her life out of ten. After all the changes she had made recently there were lots of eights and nines on the page that made her realise how far she had come. When it came to scoring money, she was in the middle of grumpily writing a big fat zero, when once again she was struck by her daughter's wisdom beyond her years.

Quietly Liza said, "Mum, you can't put a zero because we've never starved. Didn't you buy a new car last year? Oh, and we went on holiday. Twice!" Suitably chastised, she scribbled out zero and grudgingly put down a three.

Over the coming months she realised a lot about her attitude to her business and herself. Paul never told her what she should do and he asked some really thought-provoking questions. After every session though she had notes and ideas aplenty and would get off the phone excited by her business.

Paul often used his own experiences, which had been part of a real journey of challenge and triumph over adversity. She slowly began to realise that every person who owned their own business really had to have a passion. It really was, in Paul's words, 'A hero's journey'.

Ever so slowly her business gained structure while she gained confidence. Gradually she became able to speak more naturally in front of a room, or turn up for a meeting where she knew no one. She started running Paul's local networking group and although at first she was very nervous, she soon got into the flow of speaking in public and actually enjoying the experience.

Sometimes she joked too much and sometimes she forgot what she was going to say, but usually everyone laughed – with her not at her – and all the meetings ended with people driving off with a smile on their face.

It struck her that although she had fabulously used the phrase 'Fake it until you make it', she really had grown into her new self.

Sometimes the nudges the Universe gave her really did work out for the best as long as she trusted them, took a deep breath, felt the fear, grabbed the chocolate and did it anyway!

\*\*\*\*

## CHAPTER 8

Now Tabby knew who she wasn't.

She wasn't a stay at home housewife, she couldn't cook and she didn't like working for someone else. She knew she loved being in business and the person everyone saw at work was sorted, calm and collected.

So what about the real Tabby, the one on the inside? After learning of this new and exciting world was it her destiny to meet her true soul mate and live happily ever after? She had met her first husband while she was still at school, so had never had a rock and roll lifestyle. They had enjoyed nights out of course, but she had let her husband do the deciding and she had always been happy to enjoy nights in.

So where did she want to go for fun?

## TABBY TURNS THE TABLES

She had moved several times since her divorce, trying to find the perfect home for the three of them. They had had a couple of false starts, with their first home being clearly haunted. The empty grate would smell of smoke at 10pm every night despite the lilies there and even the girls felt the odd invisible wet dog brush by them. Toys would start up even when the girls were away for the weekend and she could never get used to being tapped on the shoulder – even with her new Mediumship skills!

After six months of living there, although it had been great for her spiritual development, she was exhausted by the constant noise and moving objects, so decided on a 'normal' house. So as a family they upped sticks and packed everything away into box after box. It appeared that they had accumulated endless possessions despite moving into an unfurnished house six months previously.

The house they had chosen had initially seemed perfect, being near to school and within their price range. Once they had moved in though, she started to doubt her choice.

The house was well below street level with a sloping front garden and lots of steps. It felt as if the sun never got in and although they did lots of house cleansing and candle lighting the energy never really improved. Six months later they were burgled, something she never quite got over…so they moved again.

It was time for a fresh start and Tabby thought it would be romantic and fabulous to move to the country. They chose a pretty little house in a village twenty minutes' drive from the home town she had grown up in and never left.

Her parents clearly thought she had lost the plot, so decided to forbid the move. It was at this point, aged thirty-four, as she hired the removal van regardless of the warnings, that she realised she had finally grown up.

Living in her parents' care had been amazing and Tabby knew beyond doubt that her parents were trying to protect her from a place of utter love. She also knew that she had to prove to herself that she could stand on her own two feet, that she could spread her wings and live her life her way.

Those early days in their new house were quite surreal, as she wondered what had driven her to move to a village where she knew no one. It almost felt like a reinvention of yourself is only possible when you move somewhere new, wear different clothes and dye your hair a different colour every week.

Mum and daughters had great fun in their new home, afternoons were spent playing in the sunshine and trips to school were an adventure. She really did marvel at her new self, who would drive through puddles so the girls could raise their hands in the air and squeal.

One day she decided the family was incomplete – they needed a cat. One Sunday afternoon she set off on a secret mission to the RSPCA, intent on finding a cat that needed a home and would relish endless cuddles and attention. She had assumed there would be lots of cats to choose from and that her decision would be really hard. She needn't have worried; there wasn't a single cat in all these cages that was available and good with children.

Standing at the end of the row thinking of how easy this should have been, she sighed and declared, "How come there isn't a single cat available?" In the silence that ensued she became aware of a tapping, scratching noise to her left. Beyond the barrier in the section marked 'Quarantine' there was a tiny black cat with defiant eyes and a beautiful velvet coat, valiantly scratching at the glass for all she was worth.

Immediately she asked about this little pussy cat and was told she was in quarantine but had two days to go before she could be adopted. Watching as this determined, tiny personality continued to scratch and beg for attention; she knew she had been chosen.

## TABBY TURNS THE TABLES

A week later, after the home visit had been done, Izzy arrived at her new home. At two she was tiny for her age; apparently she had been starved as a kitten. Timidly she sniffed at her new surroundings and found all the hiding places. Over the next few days she relaxed a little and her playful side showed through; a paw would strike out at her through the banister as she went down to breakfast!

She grew to understand how this little cat had learned its survival methods. Her food bowl always had to have something in it and just for good measure Izzy showed her amazing hunting skills.

One particular morning Tabby lazily opened one eye and screamed as she saw the bloody severed head of a mouse displayed on her crisp white duvet and a very smug cat. From that day on Izzy was only allowed access to the conservatory while they slept – with its wipe clean floor!

Happy days were spent with her children and evenings were spent tucked up with DVDs and home-baked cookies. The girls continued to learn how to cook new and exciting dishes rather than overwork the smoke alarm. Everyone got along fine, life flowed and the months passed by.

It was the weekends when the girls went to visit their dad that were tough. She had a great group of friends and could always arrange an evening out. There were many

3am finishes to evenings, staggering home with their stilettos in hand and lots of giggling.

She had been out for a few romantic encounters on those evenings out, but if you don't know who you are how do you know who you want to date? Her friends had fun labelling her dates – there was Migraine Boy who always cried off, then Yorkie Man who drove a lorry and Gandalf, a fellow Medium who was on the scene for a while.

Something was always missing. Every one of her dates seemed to assume she was this or that, or that she would love to be at their beck and call. One even cancelled three dates on the trot to take his mum shopping! "Is it too much to ask for someone to look into my eyes and see me?" she complained to her friend over a coffee and a cake.

So she decided to do something simple: to find her own happiness. The first evening in on her own was a bit of a challenge, despite lighting candles and playing her favourite music. It was much easier to distract herself going out than to sit in and think. So much had happened over the last few years.

She had started out with the innocent view that life would be easy, that her childhood happiness would just continue into adulthood. Was it so naïve to think this? There had been so many times when life had let her down, when she had lost the grandparents that had given her their unconditional affection and love, when she had lost her safety, her freedom and her identity.

Quietly she sat staring at a candle and started to remember the things she had gained. Sitting in front of that candle with Shanamaya supporting her shoulders, she reconnected to her inner strength, to the peace that was always there in the background. She connected to the energy of nature, asked to hear higher wisdom, agreed to listen to her own spirit and accept the healing being offered.

Layer by layer the past unfolded. Feelings, visions and realisations flashed into her mind. There was so much pain here and she wondered if she could cope with the waves of emotion that were hitting her so violently. At times her stomach lurched and her heart physically hurt, but she continued to sit with her candle.

Finally admitting the failure of her marriage and feeling the guilt that she had hidden away caused her breath to hitch and she thought she was having a heart attack. Her mind went back to having to part with Casper, her little doggy best friend, and sending him away to stay with family. She had cried a lot at the time and yet here were more tears and more pain bursting forward.

Trying to deal with a new life had meant burying her grief when her nan died. She wanted to be strong for her girls, but all the tears she had hidden away spilled out now. The times she had moved house thinking they had found a place to be happy, just to find a reason to move on again when moving house was so exhausting.

There had been so many discoveries, so many dizzy highs and crashing lows. Had the last few years really contained all this? How was it possible to bury this much emotion and not notice?

After several hours and lots of tissues, gradually and gently the tears ceased and the Universe restored balance and calm. There was a silence and a space, a place where she could just be.

She sat quietly, looking around at her home through her sore and yet new eyes. Now there was nothing to drive her on when she was exhausted, nothing to run from or hide away. There was just a place within her, a central point around which life revolved. In this centre there was peace, but also a strength that she had never known before.

Strangely enough, after this life relaxed. She still socialised, met friends and went out, but there was no pressure to always have something to do. Saturday mornings without the girls could be spent on her own, with her favourite songs on the radio.

She found that she quite enjoyed her own company, that she could watch the world around her rather than rushing from place to place. She had always been a writer, but now she had space to get ideas for poetry, to write her own visualisations and create more articles based on life.

***

Tabby continued to work on events and had a new partner in crime: Milly. Milly was a Psychic Medium and Life Coach and the pair had met during a holistic fair. Funnily, although the other event goers were dressed in black velvet or tie dye, Milly and Tabby were dressed almost identically in flowing skirts and an M&S twinset.

Although very different, they both shared similar views on life, shoes and chocolate. Their pasts had been very different too, but both had learned from their challenges and refused to play the victim, instead choosing fun and discovery. Hours were spent talking about life, about the spirit world, about being psychic and developing Mediumship.

When they talked about an events company, both of

them were very enthusiastic and jumped right in together. They had come up with events, talked about details and planned every step. Working with Milly was always a joy, her enthusiasm would shine through and on 'quiet' events it was always Milly that came to her aid and placated any potential complaints with a word or two.

Milly inspired Tabby in lots of ways. She always seemed to say the right thing to encourage her to take steps forward and she was there with the sympathy and a complete lack of judgement when she made a mistake.

She had helped her with Mediumship, pointing out ways to make the evidence from spirit more precise. Being a Medium had always been an honour for her and she was always trying to make sure her evidence was clear. Milly had been on several courses and had studied Mediumship for longer.

She was amazing in a very humble way, always striving for more detail to make her messages clearer.

Milly was also a writer. She was working on not one but four books at a time and also wrote for several magazines. Tabby loved this and mentioned her wish to be published, so when Milly read one of her articles and told her it was fabulous she also gave her the shove to send it off.

The e-mail to the editor of a local magazine was almost

an apology. It went along the lines of 'I have written this article and you probably get hundreds that are much better but I would be endlessly grateful if you would just have a quick look.'

Within hours there was a reply: it was the most beautiful, inspiring and heartwarming thing the editor had ever read and could they publish it please. She was stunned; someone wanted to publish something she had written. So she added 'published freelance writer' to her list of skills and embarked on hours lost in a creative, literary world.

It was while being immersed in this written world that Tabby made another realisation. Writing creatively sparked an even deeper connection to her intuition and allowed her heart to sing. Her visualisations became more bold and flowed into random worlds.

They were full of description and detail and it seemed like they came from somewhere else.

She would hear a line in her head while out with the girls or at work, then later be able to write the whole thing once alone. She tried her new visualisations out on friends and would be delighted when they would open their eyes and then beam a happy, contented smile that seemed to come from deep within their soul.

Once again she realised that nothing is ever lost. Every experience she had contributed to something, even if it was held dormant for years. Life and people continued to amaze her, would she ever stop learning or understanding how the Universe worked?

\*\*\*\*

# CHAPTER 9

The question of religion had always baffled Tabby.

She had been christened Church of England and gone to a Christian school. There had been plenty of trips to church to celebrate all the festivals, but she had never quite got it. She had never felt any upliftment or energy, no flashes of light, no light bulb moments.

There were lots of people in the church who did of course, and it made her giggle when the 'very religious' lady collecting the donations then spent her time in the churchyard telling tales on all her neighbours.

The last few years had told her she was a pagan of some description. Whether she was Wiccan, a Druid or a Shaman though, she wasn't quite sure. Did she have to choose? She loved the teachings of Buddhism and Taoism too, but always seemed to come back to her earthy roots.

She decided that for now she didn't need a label; she would continue to learn and experience as much as possible and talk to people that practised in different ways. As long as you had faith in something, even if it was yourself, surely that was enough?

If what you practised came from your heart and made you a kind person who cared for others then surely it didn't matter if you went to church or meditated under a tree?

It wasn't just her religious views that were changing; it seemed everything around her was shifting. What she did for a job, how she spent her days, as well as the people she had around her and what she believed in.

Her own journey had caused lots of questions among friends and family. There were some who had taken her new calling as a good excuse to make fun of her, there were others who constantly wanted a reading and yet didn't listen to anything she said. Deep down she knew that these people weren't really friends and gradually saw less of them. Mostly though, her true friends just loved her being happy and these were the people she gave her time to.

Her parents had initially been a bit sceptical of her new experiences, but time and again proof came through from the spirit world to convince them.

## TABBY TURNS THE TABLES

Tabby had received a message about her own grandfather on her dad's side that had been so precise and something that had been kept from her as she had been too young at the time. The look that went between her mum and dad was a clear sign that they were indeed believers in life after death.

Gradually, she became comfortable without a religious label and felt she had a new personality on the inside, so experimented with her wardrobe and 'look' on the outside. She was not the glamorous sort, but a host of colours had come in to her wardrobe to complement this new found zest for life. She laughed as she remembered her 'gothic' stage, when she had dyed her hair raven black and opted for black velvet skirts and lots of red satin blouses.

Eventually she realised that you only had to dress it up on the outside when you were a little unsure on the inside...the new confident Tabby could talk about her work with passion in jeans and a t-shirt!

Gradually she relaxed and was happy to be herself, happy to attend business meetings and speaking engagements alike with a quiet sense of confidence. She was keen not to appear over confident or to let her ego run riot...to get on and do anything at all you needed a bit of ego to push you forward, but she pictured her own as pinned underneath her foot, always in check.

## TABBY TURNS THE TABLES

It seemed to her that when she spoke of spirit, of people and of connection that the energy came from her heart, often creating a lovely feeling that radiated out into the whole room. Sometimes she couldn't remember what she had said afterwards, words just flowed and she would look on amazed at how many smiling faces were looking back at her.

Evenings of Mediumship were a great honour for Tabby; she never thought herself good enough so was overjoyed when she was invited. Initially she worked with Milly, learning from her experience and also her confidence. Evenings with Milly were a joy to do; they were able to create a mix of heartfelt, precise messages and an uproar of laughter.

One particular time she had read that all the TV Mediums wore red underwear, to keep them grounded while they were working. That night she was more than a little nervous, so decided she needed all the help she could get.

Half way through the demonstration Milly quietly walked behind her and tucked in the ribbon from her knickers that had been hanging out the whole time! Her face was the colour of the aforementioned underwear for quite a while after that.

It was while practising more Mediumship that her

relationship with Shanamaya continued to grow and she learned to trust his words and work with him. She had been for a regression workshop with a fantastic hypnotherapist called Brian that had led to her learning more about her connection with Shanamaya. Brian had regressed a room of a hundred people, taking them back to their childhood, to their birth and then to a past life.

For Tabby the past life was in Native America, where she had been the daughter of a tribe Elder. She was a keen archer and horsewoman; she saw images of herself riding bareback across the plains. When she was twenty-seven there had been a great war between tribes and her twin brother, Shanamaya, had been sent to fight. Being a girl she hadn't been allowed, despite her great protests.

The part where her twin brother had been brought back injured and died in her arms had been so poignant, as if it was happening to her in present day. Tears streamed down her face as she relived this pain. After this she had gone on to create peace between the tribes through the tribes' women and had died in peace surrounded by her family at a ripe old age.

Was that why in this life she had woken on her twenty-seventh birthday feeling forlorn and had hated that whole year? Was that why when she had a picture drawn of her guide she had initially thought the artist had just painted her as an American Indian man?

As a young girl she had often asked her mum if she was a twin, as she felt a part of her was missing. Could it be this twin energy that had survived through lifetimes, allowing her to work with Shanamaya in such an instinctive way?

There had been so many synchronicities, visions and knowledge given to her that she didn't question her messages any more. Signs and intuition had served her well in her own life, allowing her to make huge changes for the better and to walk away from people and circumstances that were going to end in tears.

When people asked for readings now she refused any requests to 'prove it'. She would calmly state that she knew that guidance and inspiration was available to everyone. If at any time a connection couldn't be made she would simply waive any payment; she firmly believed herself capable, but maybe not capable of reading for everyone on the planet, any day at any time.

Readings were a mix of her own energy, her client's energy and the connection to spirit. Sometimes there were blocks that made connection tricky. This had happened a few times out of hundreds of readings, so it wasn't something that concerned her, although she always tried her best.

It was funny – the more 'spiritual' she got the more human she considered herself. As her confidence grew she became quieter. She was drawn to work with others of a similar quiet nature; it saddened her to discover that some of her gurus and heroes talked the talk, but were far from walking their walk.

For the few who were full of ego and 'showbiz' though, there were hundreds that she met who were passionate, full of love and genuine. She was honoured to have such amazing friends with a shared quest of loving life and helping others.

****

## CHAPTER 10

While out driving one day Tabby couldn't help but marvel at life.

When she had been young everything seemed like it was all mapped out, no surprises or changes, just following a plan that to this day she hadn't quite understood.

When young she had loved excitement and fun, yet had unconsciously moved herself into a life of responsibility and predictability as she grew older. Most of the huge occasions in her life had been undertaken without any real thought of there being another way, a better choice or more excitement.

If at the age of twenty-two someone had told her that within a decade she would be divorced, living in a different town, with her own business and that she would be a Psychic, Medium and Holistic Therapist, she would have laughed in their face.

Not in a rude way of course, she had been brought up to be polite and respectful, the very idea would have just been too fantastical to contemplate.

So many changes had happened in the last few years. Her pagan ways meant she really felt connected to the planet now and could love every day and every season for its natural beauty.

She was more in touch with her own intuition and felt able to make good decisions or wait for the right moment. There were a few mistakes over the years, but usually they were at times when life was really busy, or when her unending optimism refused to give in to reality. She realised with a smile on her face that she loved her life.

That didn't mean there weren't ups and downs any more, of course there were. It just seemed that she bounced back from the downs and could really enjoy and make the most of the good times. Frequently in her mind she would take a snapshot of life and stop to admire the beauty of a sunrise, the freshness of the rain or the glow of a flower.

Her thoughts turned to her girls. They had coped so well with all the changes, from years of everything being the same to years of constant change. Through all of their moves her girls had gone along with their mum even when they were unsure, as she searched for the right place for her family to be happy.

Eventually she had come to know that if you are happy on the inside your surroundings usually matched, but she had got to know that by experience.

At the end of her marriage she had been switched off.

She had gone through the motions of life, but a part of her was closed down to protect itself from any more hurt. She winced at the thought of her girls having half a mum.

Now though, when they were all together, there were giggles, cuddles and a relaxed atmosphere. As the mum she rarely had to pull rank, but when she did it wasn't for long and she would usually make a silly face or say something outrageous to break the tension.

She had kept her daughters at the same school during all their moves, trying to keep their education steady. Lauren had always struggled at school; it seemed the education system didn't know how to cope with someone who wasn't naughty, just different.

Lauren had fallen down the stairs at three and from that point the laid back, contented angel who was happy to sit and play had sped up, acting as if she had been drinking buckets of coffee. Her sleep was interrupted, her concentration was zero. She had been diagnosed with

Attention Deficit Disorder, but not to an extent where she could get any real help, just the offer of a prescription for Ritalin, a medication that horrified Tabby.

Why would a child benefit from being given a drug to make them docile and artificially mask their symptoms? Surely some extra tuition and the support and understanding to cope was a better alternative?

Lauren was often bullied by the children at school and sometimes by the teachers too. Even at six-years-old an incensed teacher declared that Lauren had 'lied' about having her dinner when she hadn't had it at all.

It really didn't take a scholar to work out that it hadn't been a deliberate lie; Lauren had been so scared by this tyrant of a teacher looking daggers at her that she had simply said what she thought the teacher wanted to hear.

Tabby tried her best to help her daughter and there had been so many visits to the head of year, head of school, etc. Nothing seemed to work though, so she and Lauren had just vowed to get through it together. Lauren had outside help when she could and again, holistic therapy worked its magic giving Lauren some tools to help her cope.

Liza had always got on well at school, apart from some early squabbles at senior school. She always found homework easy, mostly completing it before the end of the lesson and was often weeks ahead of the class. Tabby wasn't quite sure where Liza got her love of sciences, but she was great at all her subjects and parents evening was always a joy.

Liza's struggles were with her emotions. Tabby had kept her silence when her ex-husband had rejected their beautiful second daughter, her level of shock meant that she hadn't even told her parents.

When she left, her ex had leaned heavily on his daughters, opting to share his every emotion with them. Lauren was too young to notice really, but Liza would carry the burden and try to solve his problems. It was as if he had gone from moaning at his wife to moaning at Liza and Tabby would wince when she heard the level of detail he shared with a child.

It was during one of these sharing sessions that he admitted he hadn't wanted Lauren when she was born as she was a girl. Lauren was eight years old at this point and Liza eleven, so no age to be told such a thing. Tabby had never forgiven her ex-husband for this; she could forgive everything that happened to her, but nothing that hurt her children.

The girls came home that day and asked her if this was true – what could she say? They also told their nan about this, so she had to tell her parents the truth about something she was hoping she could keep to herself. She had hoped her children would never know about this, but now the truth was out.

From that point everything changed for Liza.

Her dad was no longer a hero, but a monster that had rejected her lovely sister. She became overprotective of Lauren, angry and resentful of her dad and after a few years of struggling to reconcile her emotions she refused to go to see him.

Of course he was full of anguish and outward displays of emotion, but refused to take any blame, instead insisting that his daughter had been turned against him by Tabby.

All she could do was quietly support her children, to be there with extra cuddles and to make their time with her as fun and easy as possible.

There were a few extra spontaneous trips shopping and some additional pizza and film nights together as she did her best to compensate for any pain her girls may be feeling. She tried to create as many happy memories as she could and loved hearing the laughter that ensued.

She had learned long ago that her ex held a very different view of the happenings of life and it would do no good to try to convince him that he was wrong. She had used up so much energy trying to placate and support him over the years to no avail. Her years of working with spirit had made her understand that you can't choose what anyone else does, but you can always choose how you react. It was hard to do, but she had to let it go.

Her reaction was to continue to be strong, to learn and to experience. She chose to make her daughter's lives full of opportunity, to show them that anything is possible if you want it badly enough.

Her daughters were indeed amazing; they had come through so much and yet for the most part laughed and enjoyed life. They were always there for each other, all three of them – they had built a girlie home that was their castle full of fairy lights, packet made cakes and burnt pizzas and they loved it!

Since being on her own she had taken charge of her finances. As a married couple she and her ex-husband had earned a good salary each and yet there had never seemed to be money for extras. Now she was bringing in one salary and a self-employed one at that, but it was amazing what had been possible.

When she decided to move to the country her new house had been considerably cheaper than the one in the city, so she had a lump sum left over. Imagine her glee when she realised that the car she had been dreaming about could be hers. Soon she and her girls were having great fun in their brand new yellow Mini Cooper.

She had never had a new car before, so she lovingly chose white bonnet stripes, heated white wing mirrors and a really cool interior. Hours were spent driving around the country, the girls' favourite CDs being played and the car full of happy singing voices. The fact that she now had her first ever speeding ticket seemed a small price to pay!

The extra cash also bought some amazing holidays. She always talked of wheelchair moments: the memories you are left with when you are old and housebound that will make you smile from morning until night.

Tabby and her friend Charlotte had a bucket list of all the things they intended to do, from completing a half marathon, to paragliding, to getting wrongly arrested. Charlotte had so far managed a CID caution, but she refused to accept this as a completion of her mission!

The family had spent a fun-filled fortnight in Mexico, along with her parents, brother and niece. Puerto Vallarta was idyllic and the girls thrived on adult company and fun pool games. They had an all inclusive package, so on arrival she had told the girls about their wrist bands and said that if they showed these they could eat and drink what they liked.

You can imagine the uproar at breakfast when a very

cute, blonde-haired Lauren came struggling back to the table with a plate piled high with doughnuts – thirteen in all!

She soon got the idea though and chose less the next day, but spent happy afternoons with a blue mouth from endless slush puppies!

They had a fantastic experience swimming with dolphins, where again Lauren stole the show. There was a dolphin calf that weighed in at 500lbs and he soon noticed that Lauren had a short attention span.

When her attention wandered, he would swim behind her and nudge her shoulder, causing her to shriek and the family to laugh. He would swim off with a real smile in his eyes then wait for her to wander again and repeat his nudging. The intelligence, beauty and grace of these animals was truly amazing and Tabby's eyes glistened with tears as she connected with them one by one.

The holiday had been amazing; with Liza learning yet more Spanish and looking like a native with her dark hair, piercing serious eyes and glorious olive skin that would glow with even the slightest exposure to the sunshine. Lauren came home a delicate sun-kissed peach, her blonde hair now nearly white.

Their next trip was Florida. They hired a van that could have belonged to the A-Team as there were so many of them and so many bags. With her brother driving, her navigating and her parents giggling along with the girls they had hours of fun travelling between theme parks.

It was on this holiday that she made a surprising realisation; she was no longer scared of rollercoasters.

Her dad had always egged her into going on the tallest and scariest of rides by daring her – something she couldn't walk away from. So she and her dad would queue and she would sweat and feel sick until the ride was over.

This time all that had changed – she was the one seeking out the worst of the worst and her dad was now showing apprehension. He admitted that he'd always been scared; he had just always tried to get her to reach out of her comfort zone.

Could it be that the challenges she had faced in life recently had made her more adventurous in other areas too? Either way she enjoyed her new found freedom and constantly found more and more rides to tease her dad on to.

And so every month that the mortgage got paid, the girls got the things they needed and she lived her passion. Sometimes life was tricky and there were moments when she would wonder where the money was coming from for this and that. At times she felt tired of working for herself;

it could be lonely and all too easy to be distracted into putting the washing on or meeting a friend for coffee.

On the whole though, she had a good work ethic and being her own boss meant she could take her children to school and be there to collect them at the school gate. She could be there when they were sick and give them more support when they struggled.

When she was inspired she could stay up past midnight working on a new idea, or rise early when a dream contained the content for a new visualisation.

The writing she loved so much never came between the hours of 9am and 5pm, so she would go with the flow, something that appealed to her floating, Piscean nature.

During those late night sessions, her mind would sometimes wander to her love life. Her recent happiness meant she now met less people with their own agendas and her intuition allowed her to spot people who were on her wavelength. She had more friends and contacts so her social calendar was always lively.

She had never pictured herself being alone, she longed for someone to come along and join in with her happy life. She felt that she had failed in her first marriage and accepted her part in its failure.

It would be lovely to marry again and share adventures with someone who would understand her frailties, encourage her in challenges, but most importantly she desired someone who would look into her eyes and really see who she was. Someone who would know when she was hiding her sadness and who would allow her to be herself.

****

# CHAPTER 11

"Ugh!" was the only sound that Tabby could manage.

It was the morning after her thirty-fourth birthday and she was dying. Her mouth felt like a desert, her head throbbed and her stomach lurched every time she moved. She was sure the heating was off and then groaned at the hot and cold sweats of a mammoth hangover.

Was it possible to feel this ill unless you were actually dying? Maybe the kebab had been off or maybe the glass had been dirty?

She had never been much of a drinker, but the past couple of years had re-introduced her to partying and alcohol. She was a mum at twenty so had never really been the partying type until her recent new lease of life. There had been countless evenings out with friends of late and early mornings tiptoeing home with her high heels in her hand. She loved the nights, but it was the hungover mornings that hurt.

Last night had been great, a birthday celebration that had entailed partying, dancing, drinking and more dancing. She and her friends had enjoyed their night, until the accepted ten to two frenzy, where the virile single alpha males decide that they must endeavour to take someone home with them.

The particular alpha male that approached her hadn't read the classic signals given off by their group not looking for male company. She had often been accused of flirting with men and woman alike, but really she just couldn't disguise her like of people.

Last night was a classic case of getting it wrong though; when approached she happily chatted away lost in her own world, unaware of the hidden agenda. So when Alpha Male told her he was a New York journalist she didn't recognise the showmanship. When Alpha Male complimented her on her dress she deflected the compliment by saying how little she had paid for it – approach number two went unnoticed. When Alpha Male invited her back to his flat for sex, she must have looked very shocked indeed!

The following morning she had gathered enough gusto despite her hangover to still be incensed. "That's it!" she crossly declared. "If there isn't a man out there who is a prince not a frog and someone who wants to love me for who I am rather than a notch on the bedpost then I mean it, I'm joining a nunnery!"

After three more coffees, being sick and several sips of water the hangover fog lifted enough for her to remember to check her diary. Her brother John had his birthday party tonight and she had promised to go.

After a fry up, a sleep and some trudging around, she found something to wear and comfortable boots. Her feet had always been temperamental and could only just stand one night of partying in heels, definitely not two!

When she was sure all of last night's alcohol had seeped out of her system she drove over to her brother's armed with a sleeping bag, a bottle of 'hair of the dog' wine for getting ready and a bag full of makeup to hide any remnants of over indulgence.

She could at least relax a little tonight; John had never been a drinker so had opted for a Chinese takeaway, a few drinks at the local pub then a dance in the disco held at the local bowling alley.

Initially she had groaned at her brother's plans, but after her own wild night she was quite pleased they were staying local and tame. Her friend Hannah was coming out too, so once at the restaurant the party mood kicked in and she found she could enjoy a glass or two of wine.

She and John had always been close and shared a sense of humour generally lost on others. John had recently been divorced too and had a young daughter. She had shared many a social occasion with her brother and so knew most of John's friends. As people arrived she said hello to and recognised everyone in the restaurant, except for Seb.

Apparently Seb had known John for fifteen years and they had shared many a night out together, along with the rest of the friends that she already knew.

Seb sat opposite Tabby and Hannah and soon they were all laughing together. It seemed John's lack of drinking ability was legendary, so they all shared a giggle and with a cheeky smile she showed the group the picture of John's Horlicks jar, much to her brother's embarrassment!

The night progressed, the wine flowed and soon they were at the bowling alley. Seb had whisked her off to the dance floor, after holding out his hand and gazing at her with a particularly mischievous look that made her heart flip. They danced, they giggled…and was it her imagination, or was this the kind of fun she had been lacking of late?

At midnight John came over. "Bedtime Sis!" he

declared. "John, it's your birthday!" she replied. "This place closes at 2am so please don't tell me you are giving in already!" It seemed that was the case as John raised one eyebrow, a look she knew meant there would be no changing his mind.

Apparently though, she had a knight in shining armour. "I'll escort your sister home, mate," Seb said. John shook his friend's hand, offered his thanks and hugged his sister goodnight.

When they were out of earshot Seb leaned in close. "It may be my home though." He grinned. Normally this would have sent her running after her brother, but there was something in those twinkling, deep blue eyes that made her feel that she was safe.

*** 

Tabby couldn't believe how happy she felt.

Her new boyfriend it seemed had no end to his talents. He could guess where she wanted to go, he knew what gifts to buy that suited her perfectly and he got on great with her parents. Before every date her stomach would flip with such violence and excitement that she would bend double. Who was this man who made her toes curl up with delight and how come they had never met in the last fifteen years?

No subjects were barred; they talked endlessly about their history, their families and their lives. She had admitted how sick she felt when she had woken up at Seb's with a monster hangover, but his confession beat hers.

When waking up the only name Seb could remember from the previous evening was 'John's Sister.' Luckily another friend was sleeping downstairs and he had been able to remind him of her name. Seb's genuine nature shone through here and the pair laughed for hours at their haphazard first date.

The couple shared many similarities: both had been married for years, both had two children and both had divorced around the same time. Both had enjoyed single life, although Seb travelled for work a lot and so had partied further afield and for longer periods of time it seemed.

His view of travel was so casual; he could pack in twenty minutes and would often not know where he was going until he got to the airport. She had travelled a fair bit, but only after careful planning and days of choosing shoes!

Seb's work trips were something she had to get used to, as her family and friends had always been around her. Seb would whizz around packing and then be off with a kiss, a bear hug and a twinkly, "Missing you already!" Being a serial texter, she would send text messages through the day and get a little twitchy when a reply didn't ping back in seconds.

She wasn't sure if it was a girl thing, this needing a response, or just years of conditioning, but Seb would always call when he took a break, making her eyes light up and her heart leap as the affection poured down the phone from thousands of miles away.

Their first holiday had been a raucous affair, with lots of drinking but more importantly hours of giggling. She couldn't remember when she had been quite so happy. They liked the same things, they finished each other's sentences and they were never stuck for something to say.

Seb had got on great with the girls too, always just being their friend and never stepping in as 'Dad'.

Soon though their affection for him became very clear and she would stand by mocking outrage as her daughters walked straight past her and asked Seb's advice on clothing, boys and life.

They had all gone away for a weekend camping trip, when Seb had spectacularly rescued their toilet roll from the clutches of a fox that snuck into their tent under cover of darkness. The girls had squealed and giggled and could not get back to sleep, until they moved their sleeping bags in to sleep beside Seb and their mum – it was all a little squashed!

They spent evenings eating fish and chips on the quay and daytimes walking along the beaches. Seb would lend his coat when they shivered, open the doors for them and let them try anything on his plate that they hadn't eaten before.

Gradually the girls started to see Seb as a problem solver and someone who just wanted to help, never wanting to lean on them or get their sympathy.

Her friends also took to Seb, who flattered them all with a cheeky comment and a wicked grin. Her boyfriend had a reputation for being a mischievous daredevil and would always be up for a laugh.

He also kept her guessing; if he didn't want to go somewhere then he wouldn't – particularly if the invite was to someone's wedding. "I hate weddings!" he would exclaim. Quietly she hoped this didn't mean another one of his own, but Seb remained resolute that he would never marry again. She often aired her opinion that she intended to get married again, but quietly thought that it would only ever be to one man...

The pair shared their time between houses depending

on whether she had the girls. Tabby and her girls had recently moved to Bristol to be closer to their friends and had a lovely semi-detached house.

Their home was filled with even more fairy lights, Buddhas, angels and décor that ranged from royal purple to mint green. The fridge was always empty and the freezer filled with microwave meals as her legendary cooking skills had not improved with age!

She had become fiercely independent over the years and was very proud of her achievements as a single mum. It pleased her to see how life had changed from being misunderstood and controlled to being free and happy.

Seb's boys lived with him too, so he understood perfectly when she was needed, or when last minute she had to invite him over instead of going out.

Although it was obvious to everyone around them that the couple were deeply in love, the phrase "I love you" had yet to be said, unless on a night out after a beer or three! The fun side of their relationship was clear to see and she worried that perhaps this was just fun to Seb.

One day she shared this with a friend, who just raised one eyebrow and said, "Have you noticed how he looks at you?" It seemed Seb's friends had noticed too. "Dancing Seb" had been a legend among the single males and most nights someone would come up to her and say, "What have you done to him?"

Among Seb's many talents was an amazing ability to cook, which she discovered after being invited to dinner. Expecting a bottle of wine and a takeaway, the shock must have been clearly visible when she arrived to chilled champagne in an ice bucket, an immaculate table set in black and red, dauphinoise potatoes, homemade everything and a strawberry gateau to finish.

Everything was cooked to perfection; the timings were perfect and to her amazement Seb was relaxed and happy throughout the whole affair. Any past kitchen attempts for her had been filled with frustrated sighs, sweating and last minute salvage attempts to rescue burnt offerings.

The evening was enjoyable and would have been amazing, had she not said the words, "I'll cook for you next time…"

And so the date was set, Seb was happy with the invite and she had this ominous sense of foreboding. "You did what!" was all Terri could say when Tabby shared her news.

"Why would you do that when you know you are rubbish at cooking? You know I love you, but this isn't one of your finer decisions."

"I know!" she wailed. "But it was such a lovely evening and everything was romantic and lovely and I just wanted it to happen again!" Luckily Terri was a very good friend and a plan was hatched.

On D-Day Terri turned up armed with lots of strange objects that Tabby didn't recognise. Apparently there was more to the art of cooking than she had realised. Like magic soon her kitchen was awash with the smells of herbs, spices and of slow cooking chicken, and there was a lot of giggling as her friend listed all the ways she could repay this gesture of love.

At last it was all ready, the tagine was in the oven and all was well. "Right then, off you go and make yourself look gorgeous, you've got two hours before this is done and then all you have to do is make the couscous, easy peasy!"

Seb arrived armed with the most beautiful flowers and the evening started perfectly. The soup that a well-known company made was beautifully passed off as her own recipe and she wafted off to the kitchen for the main course.

The simmering chicken and apricot dish looked amazing as it came out of the oven and she surreptitiously read the couscous instructions before sticking the pan on the heat. In an instant there was chaos as the 'easy-peasy' couscous welded itself to the bottom of the pan and started to emit the stench of burning that she knew so well.

It was at that point of course that Seb wandered out and offered to help. Standing seductively between the domestic God himself and her burning ruins she beamed her best smile and shooed Seb back into the lounge with the ploy of pouring more wine.

Her thoughts then turned to the salvage operation. Carefully she managed to scoop the non-burned contents of the saucepan on to the plates and dowsed the rest to dampen down the smell. Taking a deep breath and plastering a calm smile on her face she headed out to the dining table.

It was only after a few glasses of wine that she could contain herself no longer and confessed to her inability to cook and the charred offerings that lay in the kitchen!

Time seemed to pass so quickly these days, what with a business to run, teenagers to organise and Seb's trips away. Life was relatively calm and easy now that everyone had settled into a routine.

There were the everyday ups and downs of parenthood and the odd frustration as a plan went awry, but generally life was good.

At a recent event she had met a new circle of business associates and some great plans were hatched for running some new events. She had spent her days with her mind full of ideas about evenings they could hold, venues they could hire and the fun they would all have.

It felt as if now was the time to venture out a bit more and to try new things. The date had been set for their first Psychic Supper and she couldn't wait.

Seb's boys were growing up a lot now and there was talk of David joining the army. Matthew had recently moved away to University too and so the house was much quieter these days – and there were a lot less machine loads of football kit!

Snuggled up after another giggle-filled, relaxing weekend she was musing about how with the boys moving on it would be easier to move in together. Wouldn't it be great to have one lot of bills each month and no more travelling to and fro with weekend bags?

She had often wondered how her first marriage had gone so wrong and she and Seb were so happy all the time. She couldn't wait to wake up and see his smiling face every morning.

The comments were made while watching a movie and she contentedly smiled as Seb didn't say much – she loved how he got so involved in movies.

After a few drinks the next Wednesday Seb drove her home and was strangely quiet – he really could do with catching up on some sleep, she thought. As they pulled onto the drive her heart started to pound as Seb gently took her hands in his and turned his pained eyes to meet hers.

It seemed he loved her very much, she was his best friend in the world and he would always love her, but they would have to part. She deserved a man who would marry her and make her happy and Seb would never marry again. "I am going to die a lonely old man and you deserve better than me," Seb said.

She couldn't really remember what she had said as she got out of the car; all she knew was that she needed to get inside while her legs still worked. Somehow she got in the house and managed to put a steely phone call in to Charlotte before the tears started to flow.

Her girls were fantastic as they hugged her, took care of themselves and kept their concerned glances between them. Thankfully it was half term so there was no school run to do.

In shock she sat in the kitchen, still in her dressing gown. Her emotions would range from a glassy stare feeling numb to floods of tears and a sickening feeling in her stomach so fierce it made her wretch.

## TABBY TURNS THE TABLES

Today, at 2pm, she had an interview for an accountancy job at a local company. At 2pm precisely this tear-stained, jabbering, shocked wreck had to be in a suit and full of accounting knowledge and confidence. At 12pm she was sitting on the kitchen floor, still in her dressing gown being text coached by friends and hugged by her children.

At 2pm sharp, suited and booted she calmly walked up to the office of the shredding company and plastered a smile onto her face. The smile stayed intact and her glasses that she reserved for such interviews beautifully hid her puffy eyes. By 2.15pm with a new job under her belt she drove away and it was at this point that the tears resumed their silent journey down her face.

That night Seb came to collect the papers that he had left in her handbag. The following day the satnav that she was borrowing decided to stop working so she had to return this to Seb. The day after that they had agreed to attend a dive club social and had decided to still go as friends. It seemed as if the Universe was conspiring to keep the two in contact, but Seb never discussed their situation.

He still held her hand and gave her that amazing smile of his, but behind it there was so much sadness that remained unspoken.

How could this be happening? She had no clue where this sudden change of heart had come from after two years of blissful dating. When she had phoned Seb's best friend for clues there were none – Seb hadn't even told him of their split.

It seemed that no one else knew, so she felt as if she were living a complete, heart-wrenching lie. Could her instincts have been so wrong? Had she just been reading everything with rose-tinted spectacles on and making up signs? She couldn't believe this was so, but still the separation and lack of explanation continued.

It always amazed her how resilient human beings could be. During huge trauma and horrendous physical heart pain she was able to do the school run, learn her new job and keep the house tidy…well a bit tidy!

Her latest event had been fantastic and she had delivered her very first solo platform Mediumship message without Milly holding her hand.

From the outside her life was going from strength to strength, but on the inside there was turmoil, tears, heartache and bewilderment. How could this be happening? How could life work out like this? How could he calmly walk away and appear to be getting on with life after their two years of happiness while the physical pain literally ate away at her heart?

She had no opportunity to get answers to these questions as Seb never talked about their relationship. They had a planned weekend away as part of a group and had decided to go as friends, but the weekend was full of torture for her. On one hand Seb was chatting, holding her hand and appearing normal, but their beach walks held a chasm of pain between them and the bed they still shared was full of loneliness, silent tears and utter frustration.

On the evening they arrived another couple announced their engagement – she only just managed to get to the bathroom before she was physically sick…how could life be so cruel?

At last the weekend was over and she decided that she needed to get a grip on her life.

She had talked to an astrologer friend and he had said that for three weeks there was a Mercury Retrograde happening so communication would be difficult. He had given her a three week window in which he said he felt they could sort this out, maybe.

Those three weeks were about to end the following weekend, but she could be patient no longer.

Even though it hurt and she didn't understand, she needed her life to keep going for her own sake and that of her girls, who must be sick of their mum bursting into tears at random moments.

A song had come on while they were having a cuppa on a shopping trip a few days ago and two small hands had gently taken hers under the table as her tears and pain spilled out yet again.

So gradually she began reinventing herself. First she dyed her hair a pure, shiny raven black and got her hair cut. Then she purchased a bright red, rather short kilt. She had always power dressed when being bullied years ago and this technique seemed to work.

The songs that had initially started the tears falling, she could now sing through – even if it was in a forced and loud voice. She booked herself onto a one day Vertical Reflexology course too – her new business was going well and she decided to develop her Reflexology skills further.

The following Wednesday, while out with friends, she took a deep breath, gathered her strength and quietly told a few people that she was no longer with Seb. She asked her friends to carefully pass the news on, but could not contain her surprise as she had three dinner invitations!

It could have been her imagination, but she thought she saw a pained look flash across Seb's face, but he was silent on the way home and she knew she was imagining it.

Dinner with anyone else was something she couldn't entertain for a second, but at least the deed had been done and life could start to move again, painful or not.

Saturday arrived and she became all too aware that her window was closing. Instead of tears and sadness she was discovering a new emotion – anger!

She had endured the worst three weeks of her life and she had decided there would be no more. Resolutely she prepared for her Reflexology day and again got suited and booted, something she was getting very good at. The day was interesting and busy, and she had carefully avoided the lunchtime chatter in case she was asked too much about herself.

As she stood at the bus stop hoping that the bus would be quick so she would have time to get ready for an evening out, her phone rang.

Later that night she was off to a party of one of Seb's friends and he wasn't going, but it appeared he had changed his mind. As her face fell, she masked her voice with a false smile that didn't get close to her eyes. Of course he should come; in fact she would pick him up – what were friends for?

As she ended the call her heart lurched yet again. Could she be brave and face a night out, pretending to be happy and carefree when her heart was bursting with pain and her life felt so empty?

Hadn't the Universe been cruel enough, giving her this happiness and then taking it away, but still leaving it within reach? The last few weeks had tested every emotion she had and she was tired of playing games without explanation. A lump grew in her throat as her emotions threatened to overwhelm her again. Why was this so hard?

From somewhere deep within she found some resolve and got ready for her evening. Her new red kilt would go perfectly with her shiny new black hair and she found her high boots – hoping for the strength to walk tall. She never wore red lipstick but she borrowed some from her girls – the war paint felt imperative if she was going to survive the evening.

She had decided to drive so that she wouldn't be tempted to drink – her emotions were wavering enough without becoming a maudlin drunk!

As she walked into the room Seb's jaw dropped as his eyes looked her up and down. There it was again, that sadness…but she was afraid that the tears would fall so she quickly stalked off in the direction of the car.

Luckily they were collecting other friends on the way so there was easy conversation and loud music to mask the tension.

As they all sat down with drinks Seb's leg touched hers. A blue spark flashed between them and she felt her heart flip. They both jumped and looked at each other – if their relationship was so wrong why was there this connection?

As the evening wore on she tried to socialise and dance with her friends as she put on her now famous smile mask, trying to not let it slip. Gradually though it became hard to maintain the energy needed for this charade, so she made her excuses and found a quiet booth away from the music.

She looked outside to her waiting car – a car that had made her so happy when she bought it but was now just a thing. The colour and vibrancy of life had disappeared and unless she was with her girls nothing made her happy. Why did she stay and torture herself – it would be much easier to drive home and hide for a while.

"Can I join you?" Seb made her jump with his request. She smiled her fake smile and he sat beside her, and again the blue flash lit up between them.

She was once again exasperated, but squashed her feelings and went for small talk.

"So, how are you?" she said as lightly as she could. "Miserable," said Seb. "I have made the biggest mistake of my life and now I've lost you." She sat frozen to the spot as finally Seb began to talk.

It seemed that her light-hearted comments about

moving in together had made Seb question everything. He had promised himself after his first marriage that he would die a lonely old man, never letting anyone get close to him or leave him vulnerable.

In the beginning they had so much fun and she had been so different to anyone he had ever met. When it dawned on him that he was falling in love he had dismissed it, until she had started to talk happy families. Being a man of his word and wanting to do the right thing he decided to release her so she could go and find someone more worthy of marriage – as if this was possible, she thought!

After their split though he had been beside himself, unable to eat or sleep and sitting panic-stricken in his car unable to go into the office. He had been listening to the same songs and they had even been to the same nightclub on the same evening – he had been downstairs while her friends had tried to cheer her up above!

The weekend away had been torture for him too, he had wanted to explain how he felt and why he couldn't be with her, but he just couldn't find the words.

Her pained expression and tears hiding behind her false smile had made it all the more difficult. He too remembered the walk hand-in-hand along the beach and had shared the mixed emotions that were so difficult to untangle.

They sat for what felt like hours talking about what had happened, each trying to understand what had been happening for the other. It was clear that they had both had a traumatic few weeks and she found her heart going out to Seb as his suffering spilled out, all her anger disappearing as she sat with her hands in his.

Sitting in the booth, she could feel the anxious gazes of their friends who had stood by helplessly watching them suffer apart.

As midnight drew closer the slow music started and Seb took her hand and led her to the dance floor. He held her close and she nestled in his arms, unsure of what was next but just wanting to savour the hug that she had pined for. Seb turned to her and stared into her eyes. "Can we start again, but on one condition?" he asked. "What's that?" she said, her heart skipping a beat as she wondered what he was going to say. "That you move in with me and marry me?" Seb said quietly.

****

# EPILOGUE

It amazed Tabby how fast life could change.

As she sunned herself on the white sand of the idyllic Mauritian beach, she finally had time to stop and reflect on her busy and much changed life. She looked fondly at her wedding band and the solitaire diamond that represented the heart they shared. Memories of so many happy times now filled her mind.

Their wedding had started with a Pagan ceremony on a misty, dew-filled morning at Thornbury Castle. It was so fitting that Freda, the very person that had started her on her new life path, should be the one to host the proceedings.

She had been amazed that Seb would also want a Pagan handfasting and the pair had great fun 'secretly' preparing their words.

## TABBY TURNS THE TABLES

During the ritual there had been shaking voices and tear-filled eyes as love and emotion spilled out into the air. A woodpecker and singing blackbird joined in their voices to add to the already charged atmosphere. This was a fairytale day filled with true love and it was everything she could have possibly wished for.

Their parents, children and best friends looked on as they became 'legally wed' with a civil ceremony in the castle library.

Standing outside the library door she froze, needing a few minutes with her dad as her breath left her body.

She had dreamed and wished for the life she was now choosing and the apprehension was proving too much. Her dad did what he did best: he made a joke and grabbed her hand a little too tightly which was the magic and courage she needed to walk through the door into the sun-filled room.

The wedding breakfast was intimate and enjoyed around an oval table. Conversation was easy and the proceedings simple – the only speech was given by the best man and Seb's former wing man, who brought a tear to everyone's eye including his own!

The evening's festivities were perfect in a different way, with hoards of 'brides and grooms' sharing the party. Once everyone had arrived and after a few drinks, she and Seb couldn't resist and nipped off to swap their clothes to really get the party started.

There were roars of laughter as Tabby sparkled in stockings and a garter only just covered by Seb's suit tails, but the show was completely stolen by Seb, dancing around in a surprisingly well-fitting dress, with his boxer shorts and black shoes on show and a bubble wrap veil that had been donated by a guest!

Over recent months there had been times when she had been at the end of her tether. Times when pain and suffering were the only things she knew and challenges that appeared to have no solution. As ever, the Universe had walked resolutely by her side, ensuring that life never got too difficult for too long, that help was never too far away. No matter what, she always learned valuable lessons and the rewards were always worth it.

****

# ABOUT NICKY MARSHALL

Nicky is an award-winning, international speaker and best-selling author. She is also a mum, nan and wife and loves nothing more than family time.

At forty, Nicky suffered and recovered from a disabling stroke – inspiring a life mission to make a bigger difference.

Nicky has an accountancy background and twenty years of helping people improve their health and wellbeing under her belt. Combining both, Nicky is a mentor, seasoned workplace facilitator and keynote speaker, inspiring people to discover their own brand of Bounce! Nicky's knowledge, knack for stressbusting, hugs and infectious laugh make her an in-demand and popular speaker.

With passion in buckets and a penchant for keeping it simple, Nicky has a unique talent in breaking down the barriers that hold people back from living a life they love.

Be careful if you stand too close – her enthusiasm rubs off!

Follow these links to connect with Nicky:

www.discoveryourbounce.com

www.facebook.com/groups/discoveryourbouncecommunity

www.linkedin.com/in/nickymarshall

Or send her an e-mail: nicky@discoveryourbounce.com

# ABOUT DISCOVER YOUR BOUNCE

Discover Your Bounce has emerged as a group of companies to provide a platform for wellbeing and inspiration, to support each other and to learn from our collective experience.

Discover Your Bounce Publishing specialises in inspirational stories and business books. We provide mentoring for authors and support from inception of your idea through writing, publishing and cheerleading your book launch. If you have an idea for a book, or a part written manuscript that you want to get over the line, contact Nicky or Sharon on the links below.

Discover Your Bounce For Business provides support for employers who want to improve the staff wellbeing, engagement, culture and performance of their business. We work with CEOs, HR Managers or department heads to deliver workshops with practical, easy to implement techniques that create instant change. As we go to print, we have worked with over 3000 employees across the globe from a variety of industries and have delivered keynotes at some fantastic international conferences and events.

My Wellbeing supports individuals through mentoring and online courses to improve their energy and vision. If your get up and go has got up and gone, get in touch and get bouncing or choose your programme at www.discoveryourbounceacademy.com.

Sharon and Nicky are available to discuss speaking opportunities, wellbeing workshops and private mentoring:
Nicky@discoveryourbounce.com
Sharon@discoveryourbounce.com

You can also find out more on our website:
https://www.discoveryourbounce.com

## TABBY TURNS THE TABLES

"It's easy to be calm on a mountain top looking out over stunning vistas, but when you are smiling amidst challenges and overwhelming circumstances, you know you have discovered how to bounce!"

Nicky Marshall

Printed in Great Britain
by Amazon